PRAISE FOR ANNAPURNA'S BOUNTY

Veena Gokhale is a talented fiction writer and a food lover. *Annapurna's Bounty* is an irresistible blend of these two great passions, combining delightful Indian legends, freshly told, with her personally honed recipes. This is a book you will want to buy twice: one to give a good friend and another to keep.

— MARIANNE ACKERMAN, novelist and playwright

A confession: I need to enjoy what I am reading, and my standards are high. Also, I'm not fond of spending more time over a stove than absolutely necessary. I was not expecting a retelling of older legends and myths, accompanied by long, ingredient-heavy recipes to be my cup of tea. I have many collections of myths on my bookshelf — although most are Greek — that I could never get through. Timeless truths are great, but I also need relatable characters and a sense of where and when. Gokhale fleshes out the archetypes in these stories in a way that feels fresh and compelling, and time and place are beautifully, vividly rendered. I could almost swear that some of these stories have an actual aroma. When I came across the recipe for dal, I was inspired to head to the kitchen and make it.

— ANITA ANAND, author of *A Convergence of Solitudes*

There is a golden vein of poetry that flavours food lore, and Veena Gokhale has mined it well. Gokhale has served up a new oral tradition: a book fit to be consumed voraciously by mind and by mouth. These ancient tales of feast and famine and fire and flood have been skillfully reworked into a tapestry that weaves myth with menu. It deserves a permanent place at our dinner table.

— GAVIN BARRETT, poet, author of *Understan*, and founder of the Tartan Turban Secret Readings

This book is ingeniously designed as a banquet for the body and the mind: each of its ten chapters offers a tale and a recipe from various eras and regions of India. Men and women, divinities, demons, and animals are the heroes of these vivid and colourful stories, over which floats the heady scent of mangoes and spices.

— FRÉDÉRIC CHARBONNEAU, author of *L'école de la gourmandise*

Lovers of Indian culture and cuisine will delight in the panoply of characters in these tales where food is the riddle, the salve, the forger of bonds, the wisdom, the life-and-death clincher. Aromatic and flavourful reading! Excellent recipes a happy bonus!

— ALICE ZORN, author of *Colours in Her Hands*

ANNAPURNA'S BOUNTY

ANNAPURNA'S BOUNTY

INDIAN FOOD LEGENDS RETOLD

VEENA GOKHALE

DUNDURN PRESS

Copyright © Veena Gokhale, 2025

All rights reserved. No part of this publication may be reproduced, stored in a retrieval system, or transmitted in any form or by any means, electronic, mechanical, photocopying, recording, or otherwise (except for brief passages for purpose of review) without the prior permission of Dundurn Press. Permission to photocopy should be requested from Access Copyright.

All characters in this work are fictitious or are used fictitiously. Any resemblance to real persons, living or dead, is purely coincidental.

Publisher: Meghan Macdonald | Acquiring editors: Julia Kim & Kwame Scott Fraser | Editor: Julia Kim
Cover and interior designer: Laura Boyle
Cover image: border: shutterstock/artistsayeed; Sun and Annapurna illustration by Laura Boyle

Library and Archives Canada Cataloguing in Publication

Title: Annapurna's bounty : Indian food legends retold / Veena Gokhale.
Names: Gokhale, Veena, author
Identifiers: Canadiana (print) 2024047029X | Canadiana (ebook) 20240470338 | ISBN 9781459754591 (softcover) | ISBN 9781459754607 (PDF) | ISBN 9781459754614 (EPUB)
Subjects: LCSH: Food—India—Folklore. | LCSH: Folklore—India. | LCSH: Legends—India. | LCSH: India—Social life and customs. | LCGFT: Folk literature. | LCGFT: Legends.
Classification: LCC GR305 .G65 2025 | DDC 398.20954/0764—dc23

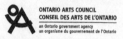

We acknowledge the support of the Canada Council for the Arts and the Ontario Arts Council for our publishing program. We also acknowledge the financial support of the Government of Ontario, through the Ontario Book Publishing Tax Credit and Ontario Creates, and the Government of Canada.

Care has been taken to trace the ownership of copyright material used in this book. The author and the publisher welcome any information enabling them to rectify any references or credits in subsequent editions.

The publisher is not responsible for websites or their content unless they are owned by the publisher.

Printed and bound in Canada.

Dundurn Press
1382 Queen Street East
Toronto, Ontario, Canada M4L 1C9
dundurn.com, @dundurnpress

*Dedicated to the Annapurnas of all genders,
who nourish mind, body, heart, and soul;
to people who find books nourishing;
and to my mother, Pramil, who is an Annapurna.*

One cannot think well, love well, sleep well,
if one has not dined well.
— Virginia Woolf, *A Room of One's Own*

CONTENTS

1. **LAND OF MILK AND SUGAR** 1
   Ash Reshteh 15
2. **PARVATI BAI AND THE BANDITS** 19
   Parvati Bai's Rassa 31
   Goda Masala 35
3. **THE EMPEROR WHO LOVED MANGOES** 37
   Mango Lassi Akbari 51
4. **THREE GRAINS OF MUSTARD** 53
   Carrot-Radish Salad 67
5. **ANNAPURNA'S SOUP KITCHEN** 69
   Goddess Parvati's Bengali Khichari 87

INTERLUDE 91
   "The World's Oldest Curry" 95

6. **DO THE RIGHT THING** 97
   Mandakini's Dal 115
7. **THE FISHERMAN AND THE SORCERESS** 119
   Avial 131
8. **CHEF WILLIAM AND CAPTAIN TYRANT** 135
   Chef William's Mulligatawny Soup 149
9. **THE CRIES OF ANIMALS** 153
   King Vajradev's Paal Payasam 167
10. **THE TRAVELS OF SANBUSAK** 171
    Veena's Karanjis 201

AFTERWORD 205
ACKNOWLEDGEMENTS 213
ABOUT THE AUTHOR 215

LAND OF MILK AND SUGAR

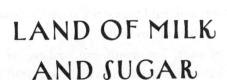

Characters
Arman, our hero
Dinaz, his grandmother
Farhad, his grandfather
Mardan, his father
Bijan, his uncle
Neda, his mother
Jadi Rana, a king

I, Arman of Sanjan, grandson of Farhad of Baqat, give this story into your safekeeping, to memorize, recall, and transmit at will and as needed, acknowledging as well that tales are told simply for sheer enjoyment and the comfort of sharing.

My resourceful grandmother Dinaz suggests that I write my story down on lengths of bleached cloth using a fine reed pen from the western lands and an ink block from the eastern lands, both procured by my father, Mardan, who is a trader. He gave them to me on my twenty-first birthday. My grandmother, unschooled and unlettered, is very proud that I can read and write and that I am a scribe at the king's palace. She would like to show off my skills.

But why write? The mouth, ears, and eyes are enough. A storyteller's expression changes like clouds shifting in the sky — his voice murmurs, now a thin stream of water, now a thunderous roar. His eyes speak as eloquently as his dancing hands — nor is his body still. Is it any wonder that his words get imprinted not just on our memory but also on our hearts?

Let us begin. Who am I, and why do I have a story to tell?

I was born in Baqat, a faraway land across the waters of the Sea of Makran. I am a traveller who was forced to flee my home. I had lived but ten summers when calamity fell upon my village. Our lands, ruled by kings that followed our ancient faith, Zoroastrianism, were invaded by Arabs. They asked us to convert to Islam, levied an unfair tax on us, and belittled and mistreated us in many ways. As time passed, they resorted to violence. They converted some of us into slaves and even started killing those who refused to forsake their faith. Under such conditions, many converted, some fought back and suffered the consequences, and others fled.

We are followers of Zartosht, who was visited by Ahura Mazdā, wise lord and the highest god. Ahura Mazdā, who presides over a kingdom of justice and is the creator of heaven and earth, told Zartosht to reveal the truth to us: both gods and humans must live ethically. Our purpose is to align ourselves with Ahura Mazdā by living a life of good thoughts, good words, and good deeds.

So that we may remember these teachings and put them into practice, we pray five times a day. We can pray at home or in an open space, be it a hillside, field, or beach. When we worship Ahura Mazdā, we turn toward the Atash Varharan, the sacred flame. Fire is wisdom and darkness ignorance. The Atash Varharan, once lit, is never extinguished. Back home in Baqat, there was a brick platform that connected directly to the earth. A small fire, tended by members of our community, always burned bright, giving us inspiration and direction.

As tales of horror from the outside world started invading our village, the elders, my grandfather among them, gathered on this platform and debated while the rest of us sat and listened. The discussions went on, under cover of darkness, for many nights. Soon the debate came down to one question: Should we stay, or should we leave before being engulfed by the full indignity of Arab rule? If we left, where would we go? As the Arabs held many adjacent lands, we could be intercepted and harmed before we reached a safe haven. We had heard that there was a sea route from Gamrūn, a coastal city, to Jaladhar, a port on an island close to a land whose vastness defied imagination, which some called Hind.

A distant relative who had lived in a nearby village left for Hind via Gamrūn many years ago. He was an ambitious trader, and we heard that the move had brought him much wealth.

"Some are travellers by their very nature," my grandfather said by way of explanation.

"Some, when they start travelling, cannot stop," intoned my uncle Bijan, a small trader himself and older than my father by a few years.

My grandmother pursed her lips in disapproval. "Don't believe travellers' tales. They ride on rogue winds and are mostly make-believe, conjured up to dazzle the imagination and lure people into disaster."

Even as the discussions continued around the eternal flame, my uncle proposed that we go to Gamrūn. "Trading ports have their own rules and ways. They are all about commerce. There, different people mingle and live together without much fuss," he said.

Surprisingly, my grandmother agreed. Was she perhaps persuaded because of the recent news that my mother was with child?

How can I describe the heartbreak of leaving our home, our village, our neighbours, our land, and most of all, the sacred flame? Have you, dear listener, had to sever every single bond you cherish and cast yourself into a tremulous future that could well turn out treacherous?

LAND OF MILK AND SUGAR

On our last day, my grandmother prepared three pouches. One contained ashes from the sacred flame; the second, earth from the garden that she tended; and the third, seeds of plants she grew there. She restricted herself to chickpea, barley, eggplant, apricot, and tarragon seeds. At the last moment, she added spinach.

We travelled stealthily by donkey cart and foot with other families from Baqat who had also decided to try their luck in Gamrūn. Walking half the night, we stopped briefly during the hottest part of the day. We ate stale, dry bread, oranges, and pistachios and what we could find en route, stopping to cook a quick meal every couple of days. We arrived in Gamrūn hungry, tired, weak, and bedraggled.

Nothing could have prepared us for Gamrūn! It was very large, noisy, and busy and made of many streets — both wide and narrow — with houses of all sizes. It was populated by people dressed in all kinds of costumes, speaking in foreign tongues. Some richly dressed men went around on fine horses, and we even saw elegant horse-drawn carts. There were many shops selling food, clothes, household goods, implements for various trades, and God knows what. We did not stay long in Gamrūn. My grandmother hated the city and said simply, "Let us go on to Hind." Not everyone shared her feelings. After the initial shock, my uncle and father looked around with interest, though my mother looked uneasy.

My mother, Neda, was a dreamer who tended to forget where she was or what she was doing, sometimes missing prayer time. Raised in a once-noble family that had fallen on hard times, she could read and speak Farsi, as well as our native tongue, Avestan. She had a great memory for couplets and could also make up her own on the spot, the subjects as varied as two goats going head-to-head in the marketplace, a bride all dressed up in wedding finery, a potter casting his wares at a wheel, or a sudden spring shower.

Soon we joined a rude camp in the outskirts of Gamrūn, set up by other Zoroastrians seeking escape. We stayed close to the people from our village. While I played with the other children on the beach, supervised by older adolescents, the women cooked and cleaned, and the men investigated how to secure passage on a ship. I fell in love with the blue-grey sea, stretching to eternity, which filled me with wonder and longing.

On our last night, we clustered around a small fire that reminded us of the sacred flame back home. My grandmother drew her family aside and said, "Many challenges lie ahead. Don't let your spirit scatter or allow your mind to play tricks. Prayer is the antidote to such meanderings." As she fell silent, she looked at my mother, who cast her eyes down.

At dawn we boarded a large sailboat. I hardly slept that first night. It was so strange to lie down on a thin blanket on a slatted wooden floor that tilted one way and then the other, and to hear the sound of the waves on the open sea. Sometimes, the masts squeaked. I thought of our relative who had made this journey more than once. My grandmother managed to keep track of the days by counting prayers. When we reached Jaladhar, she declared that she had prayed seventy-five times!

In Jaladhar we were welcomed into the homes of Zoroastrians who had escaped from our lands and made this island their home. They spoke both our tongue and that of the foreigners. We also heard that some Zoroastrian traders lived on the mainland. All this would have buoyed our spirits but for the fact that my mother looked very pale and ill. Luckily, her health improved a bit after she took the herbal restoratives my grandmother brewed for her.

Soon it was time to take our next boat. The voyage to Hind would be much shorter, and a Zoroastrian priest, or *dastur*, would be with us on board, surely a good omen. On my second voyage, my new-found love for the sea was sorely tested. After a few hours of coasting along, a storm hit suddenly, turning the sea into a monster. Soon we were wet through — quivery and nauseous. The wind continued to howl and rain lashed the ship, which heaved mightily, giving the impression that it would topple over, spilling us into our watery graves.

"He's praying! He's praying for us all!" my grandmother yelled over the deafening sound and increasing confusion.

Suddenly, I saw him — a white-clad figure down on his knees, somehow steady, his hands upraised, intoning verses of supplication in chaste Avestan, beseeching God to see us through it all. He promised that if we landed safely, he would kindle the Atash Varharan, the sacred flame, and keep it going for all times. He appealed directly to the eternal flame, asking for protection. Voices rose in prayer as we all joined in. The intensity of the incantation obliterated all else. My mother, her eyes shut, with one arm around me, prayed with an ardour I had never seen before. We averted certain death through the power of prayer, a lesson I will never forget.

After the storm subsided, the crew repaired the sail, and we made our way to the coast, where we were met by a group of Zoroastrian traders. They urged us to seek asylum in this land ruled by Jadi Rana, the benevolent king, speaking well of the place and the people. Our fellow Zoroastrians helped us transport our meagre belongings on carts drawn by cows, and we made camp a little inland.

Two days later a contingent of older men, my grandfather and the *dastur* among them, went to see Jadi Rana at his opulent palace. On return they reported that the king had received them well and asked many questions about our homeland and beliefs. While he was no stranger to Zoroastrians, such a large contingent had reached his shores for the first time. We expected an edict allowing us the right to settle, but instead there were rumours that his chief minister was not in favour of such a decision. We waited, tired from our travels and hungry for a home.

Five days after the audience with the king, a senior courtier came to our camp. He carried milk in a metal can and wore a leather satchel. The man put down his belongings and asked for a table. My father immediately set one down before him. The man then extracted a goblet from his satchel and placed it on the table. He opened the milk can and carefully filled it to the brim. Bowing to us all, he said, "This is the response of my master, the king, to your request."

Exclamations arose from the crowd as he walked away. *How beautiful it is*, I thought. The goblet was covered in a motif of vines, fruits, and flowers. It shone like the moon. Then my mother, heavy with child, walked into the midst of the circle and spoke. "I believe that the king's message is this: there are already too many people in his kingdom and there is no place for us here."

The next day, six of our men went to the palace, having secured an audience with the king. It was acknowledged that my grandfather Farhad had charmed the king on their first visit, and he was selected to be the presenter. The large administrative hall of the palace, with its jewel-encrusted throne and ornate seats for dignitaries, was packed. My grandfather bowed respectfully before the king and added a second bow for the chief minister. He also asked for a table. Placing the empty goblet on it, he filled it to the brim with milk. Then he took a pouch out of his satchel and said, "I wish for someone to taste what I have here. Fear not, it is nutritious."

A courtier stepped forward, and the king nodded assent. My grandfather deposited a bit of the substance from the pouch onto the courtier's outstretched hand. Tasting it, the man declared that it was khand, local sugar, crushed fine. My grandfather looked around for a few moments, meeting the gaze of a few courtiers. Finally, he looked directly at the king, who was smiling. Extracting a spoon from his pocket, my grandfather opened his pouch again with great deliberation. He slowly put a spoonful of sugar in the milk. "Would anyone like to taste the milk now?" he asked.

"There is no need for that. It has been sweetened," said the king.

"You are so right, oh mighty one. We Zoroastrians, who have undertaken a hazardous voyage to this beautiful land because our faith was in danger, wish to tell you that we will intermingle seamlessly here, and our good thoughts, good words, and good deeds will bring sweetness to life."

No sooner were these words uttered than the king rose to his feet and started clapping. The courtiers followed suit, and the chief minister hesitantly joined in. Once the sound had died down, the king said, "I welcome you to our land. You may settle here, for I believe your promise. But we have four conditions: you adopt our language, your women wear the same garments as our women, you cease carrying any weapons, and you hold your weddings only in the evening."

The *dastur* stepped forward. "We accept your conditions," he said solemnly.

The men came home jubilant. Among much hugging and backslapping, some tears, and many laughs, the demand rose to hold a feast. The women started cooking and concocted a delicious stew with the vegetables, meat, herbs, and spices that the Zoroastrian traders contributed. They also made homestyle barley bread to dip in it. What a long way we had come, from nibbling on dry bread when we walked long on dusty roads that led to the sea! That night we gathered around a bonfire. We whispered about how we had heated the milk and powdered the sugar for easier dissolution. We prayed to the sacred flame, thanking it for the bounty we had received.

Next morning, some of the local women brought sweets to congratulate us. It is the custom here to "sweeten the mouth" whenever there is good news. They told us that the sweets were made by slow-cooking milk and sugar for a long time until it became a dense mass, then adding in chopped nuts and powdered cardamom. Our sugar-loving neighbours, we soon discovered, were hospitable and shared food freely in this land of plenty where the cow was sacred. Their food was different from anything we had ever eaten. Peculiarly, they liked to combine sweet and sour flavours, and many people were vegetarian.

A week after his performance at the palace, my grandfather was summoned to a private audience with the king. This time he wanted to know about our family. When the king heard that I knew Farsi, he said, "Let him come to the palace and teach Farsi to my sons. It is always good to learn new languages. And while he is here, he may sit with the princelings and absorb what he will from their teachers. Would that be recompense enough?"

Life never runs in straight lines. A few weeks later, fate tossed a large dose of bitter fenugreek into that milky goblet. My mother's labour pains started before her pregnancy came to full term, and despite the presence of experienced women, including a midwife from our community, my sister was stillborn and my mother passed away.

The months that followed were a blur. Over time the world came back into focus, and I returned to the king's palace as a teacher and student. My father — who, like my grandfather, was a potter by profession — had started labouring in a kiln in the next village, but he gave that up and took up my uncle's profession of trading. My father's eternal flame had been extinguished. Far and wide he travelled, living away from home for months on end. Some who start travelling truly cannot stop.

Thus, I was twice orphaned, and Farhad and Dinaz served as both parents and grandparents. "We lost them because we had no time to install and consecrate the sacred flame," my grandmother lamented time and again. One year after my mother and sister were no more, we were granted permission by the king to build a platform and install the eternal flame in our settlement, which we named Sanjan.

Sometimes I ask myself if I will live past twenty-six summers, for my mother saw only that many, and my sister never felt the heat of the sun on her back. Twenty-one summers have already passed, and on disturbed nights I dream of lying immobile at the bottom of the ocean. I wonder if that's where my relative who left our land for Hind lies too. For though we continued to inquire about him for years after we landed here, no one had ever heard of him.

Then I recall my grandmother's words about deceitful travellers' tales. Yet, I wish that my father, who has accumulated so many during his myriad journeys, would share them with me, but he moves in silence. I believe he says nothing in deference to my grandmother, who prefers the practicality and solidity of the here and now to the exotica of faraway lands. I wish, too, that my mother was here for so many reasons, among them to make up couplets that would refract our life through the mirror of poetry.

I must go soon, as my grandmother has announced prayer time, followed by supper. I know that I will find comfort in both. Today she is going to serve a bowl of her hearty bean soup, a family favourite, fragrant with turmeric, coriander, and cumin, as well as fenugreek and mint.

Among us all, my grandmother has flourished the most. She is well suited to this colourful land where everything is intense, including the heat and the torrential downpours during the rainy season. Everything has a high note, the food strongly spiced. Her sons have built her a fine house, and her husband is a respected leader of our community. She has cultivated her garden, which is replete with plants from our native land, as well as those from this land of milk and sugar.

And now I take your leave, having added one more thread to the ever-expanding sheath of stories. For is not all human experience intertwined, made of the same cloth, woven with threads both delicate and coarse, tough and fragile, multihued and sombre? And because we are all thus enfolded, we gain something from every story, whether it is ancient or of our time, commonplace or fantastical. These skeins connect past, present, and future, spreading across worlds earthly and celestial.

ASH RESHTEH

A greeny beany Persian stew

Vegetarian, could be gluten-free
Servings: 6 | Cook Time: 50 minutes | Level: Medium

INGREDIENTS

- 1½ tablespoons olive oil
- 2 cups Swiss chard, coarsely chopped
- 4 cups mixed, canned beans, drained and rinsed
- 1–1½ teaspoons cumin powder
- 1–1½ teaspoons coriander powder
- ¾ teaspoon freshly ground black pepper
- ½ teaspoon salt
- ¼ cup fresh parsley, finely chopped
- ⅛ cup fresh mint leaves, finely chopped, or 1 tablespoon dried mint leaves
- ½ tablespoon dried fenugreek leaves (kasoori methi)
- 2 tablespoons lemon juice (to taste)

For the garnish:

    1½ tablespoons olive oil

    2 large onions, thinly sliced lengthwise

    1½ tablespoons minced garlic

    ½ scant teaspoon turmeric powder

    2–3 tablespoons high-fat natural yogurt, per serving

METHOD
The stew:

1. In a large thick-bottomed pot, add olive oil and place on medium heat. Add the chopped Swiss chard and fry for 2 minutes. Add beans and stir well. Add cumin, coriander, black pepper, and salt. Stir well. Cook on low to medium-low heat for 30 minutes, stirring occasionally. Taste and check that the Swiss chard is cooked.

2. Add the parsley, mint, and fenugreek. At this point, you can add up to a ½ cup of water, depending on your preferred consistency. Simmer the stew for 15 minutes, stirring occasionally. Take the pot off the stove and stir in the lemon juice. Taste and adjust the cumin, coriander, black pepper, salt, and lemon juice as desired.

The garnish:

1. While the stew is simmering, add 1½ tablespoons olive oil to a nonstick pan. Turn heat to medium-high and add the thinly sliced onions. Fry the onions, stirring from time to time.

2. When the onions start browning, reduce heat to medium and add the garlic and turmeric. If mixture starts to stick, add a tablespoon of water or more as needed. Once the onions are caramelized and the garlic and turmeric are well cooked, approximately 20 minutes, take them off the heat and transfer them to a bowl.

To serve:
1. Serve the stew warm on a bed of cooked quinoa or linguine. Ladle a couple of spoonfuls of yogurt as desired and some onion garnish on top.
2. This is an excellent one-dish meal. Serve with accompaniments like olives, toasted crusty bread brushed with olive oil, and cucumber slices.

NOTES
1. The quantity of cooked quinoa or linguine will depend on whether you want the stew to be more "greeny" or more "grainy."
2. Ideally, use canned beans preserved in only water and salt. Check the salt content of the beans you buy and adjust the salt in the recipe accordingly.
3. Dried fenugreek, known as kasoori methi, is available in Indian stores. Fenugreek is bitter. Adjust quantities based on your tolerance for bitterness.
4. Ideally, if using dried mint, buy it at an Iranian grocery.

PARVATI BAI AND THE BANDITS

Characters
Parvati bai, our heroine
Sawant Rao, her husband
Lali, her husband's young cousin
Ganpat, a servant
Bhimrao, a bandit leader
Mahadev, his right-hand man

Astride horses, the bandits thunder through narrow mountain roads. Crude shotguns and bullet belts slung across their manly chests are their badges of honour. The sound of hooves and high-spirited neighing reverberates through the valley. The ground shakes. Dust clouds swirl in their wake. The mountain slopes are at times rocky, at times smooth, and always treacherous during the monsoons, when mudslides make passage impossible.

Tough and weather-worn, the bandits make their home in caves and rock outcrops in remote ravines, inhabiting rough and lonely badlands. Every so often, they emerge from these hideouts and enter villages to pillage and kill with impunity. They may set your hut on fire if you show the slightest sign of resistance. They strike terror in the hearts of villagers, rich and poor, feeble as well as strong.

Bhimrao is the most fearsome bandit chief of them all. Standing six feet tall, he is well built, of indeterminate age, and rarely smiles. But if perchance he does, his smile does not reach his hooded dark brown eyes. His almost-black skin is roughed up by sun and wind; his thin lips lie in the shadow of a thick, swirling moustache. A half-moon scar descends from the corner of his right eye to the edge of his lips. He is a despotic leader of a posse of thirty men.

Parvati bai and Lali are sitting on the spacious veranda with a cool red stone floor. Both wear a *nauvari*, a nine-yard saree with clever drapery, which is elegant as well as practical.

PARVATI BAI AND THE BANDITS

Unlike more restrictive women's clothing, it allows free movement in the fields or at home.

Parvati bai sits on a large armchair. It is a bit too big for her small frame and her legs dangle, but it is dear to her as part of the dowry she brought from her parents' home. She wears simple gold jewellery, and her forehead is marked by a red bindi. She frowns as she embroiders a blouse; the pattern is complicated. The blouse belongs in the wedding trousseau of her soon-to-be-married youngest sister. Laying down her work, she picks up the reed hand fan lying on the table. It's a boiling hot day.

"Why don't you join me? You'll be cooler here," says Lali from the large swing she is perched on, humming a tune. Her forehead is dotted with a black bindi. While Parvati bai's hair is done up in a neat bun, Lali sports two long braids with ribbons. A few strands of hair hang around her face.

"Must you always tease? You know the swing makes me nauseous," says Parvati bai, pretending to be cross.

"All right, all right. At least ask a maid to fan you. The breeze from a vetiver fan is so very lovely. Then I would sit with you and help with the embroidery."

Parvati bai shakes her head. She does not like asking the servants to do small things for her all day long. "Stay. I don't think you practised the stitches I showed you last week. Did you? Don't want any sloppy work."

"Of course, the embroidery must be perfect! Like anyone's going to notice if a stitch is out of line."

"I wish your cousin would be more responsible. It's hard to believe that he hasn't found a husband for you yet. My sister is two years younger and almost married. Everything I say falls on deaf ears."

"Your husband has more important things on his mind than my marriage. And I'd rather wait a while before I get caught in *lagnachi bedi*, the fetters of marriage," says Lali, laughing.

"Such cynicism! You'll just get cheekier and cheekier. Go to the kitchen and see if they remembered to bring in the papadums that were drying in the sun."

As Lali leaves, Parvati bai takes up the embroidery again. *How I will miss her when she goes to her husband's house*, she thinks. Lali, her husband's cousin, lost her parents when she was just a child and has grown up in Parvati bai's husband's family. She is his responsibility. *Our responsibility*, she corrects herself. Still, she's not wrong; marriage does impose some restrictions.

She hears the creaky garden gate opening and looks up to see Ganpat rushing in. "Bai, bai, we're done for. Lord Vithal has forsaken us!" he says, panting as he reaches her. He stands before her, turban awry, eyes showing fright.

"What's the matter?"

"I knew this would happen one day. We're cursed. Already they've attacked Ghopdi, Malve, and other villages, and now it's our turn. Only Goddess Jagdamba can save us now. Otherwise, it's the end!"

PARVATI BAI AND THE BANDITS

Parvati bai sighs. "Tell me what happened, Ganpat."

"Bhimrao is going to attack us tonight."

A sharp intake of breath; the blouse slips from her hands. Bhimrao has no fear of the law. He often sends a warning before he takes a village. "Where is Sawant Rao?" she asks.

Just then, the garden gate swings open again, and her husband comes up to the veranda. Fifteen years older than his wife, Mr. Sawant is a dignified man. His back is ramrod straight, and he speaks with quiet authority.

Parvati bai gets up and moves toward him.

"We just got the notice," he says.

"Ganpat, don't say anything to anyone. Let me and Sawant Rao have a talk first," says Parvati bai.

"I've issued instructions. The able-bodied men will get hold of sticks, sickles, machetes, whatever they can find. And we'll meet at the Jagdamba temple in half an hour. I'll take a couple of the servants along," says Sawant Rao.

"It's worth a try, but unfortunately, it's almost certain that you'll be overpowered. Let me think. I may be able to come up with something," Parvati bai says.

Sawant Rao looks keenly at his wife. She's a clever woman, but he knows there's not much she can do this time. "Close all the windows and doors and lock them as securely as possible," he says.

Parvati bai sits down on the swing, deep in thought. As he leaves the house with two young manservants, Sawant Rao calls out to her, "May the blessings of Goddess Jagdamba be with us."

"Please be careful. May God bless you all," says Parvati bai warmly.

She watches them leave, pushing the swing with her feet. The swing creaks, then starts moving back and forth. Suddenly, Parvati bai leaps off the swing. Looking decisive, she goes in search of Lali. She finds her sitting in a corner of her room, an anxious look on her fresh young face. Parvati bai takes the girl's hand. "It's going to be all right, but you must do exactly as I say. Wear your simplest saree and take off all your jewellery. Then take all the jewellery out of the safe and tie it up in a shawl. Leave the bundle on my bed. This evening, you must wait in the room behind the kitchen. Be prepared to stay there all night."

A few hours later, Bhimrao and his men ride into the village. Bhimrao looks like the commander of a conquering army. Every house stands in darkness. Windows and doors are securely shut; people have piled their heaviest objects against their doors from inside. But there is one house ablaze with lights — Sawant Rao's.

Bhimrao orders his men to surround the place and dismount. He tells them to be on guard, their rifles at the ready. Leaving four men on guard, he opens the creaky garden gate and leads the others in. The veranda is lined with lanterns and oil lamps, as if it's the great Hindu festival of Diwali. Just as he comes up to the veranda, the front door opens and Parvati bai steps out. She wears an expensive silk saree and simple gold jewellery, including her *mangalsutra*, a necklace of black and gold beads that signifies her married status. She holds a silver tray with a small oil lamp and traditional items used to greet guests. "Welcome," she calls out.

Bhimrao moves forward cautiously, pointing his gun at her. The men follow. Parvati bai smiles, doing everything in her power to keep her trembling hands from sending the tray crashing to the ground. She directly addresses Bhimrao. "You're coming to our house for the very first time, *bhau*. May I please put a *tikka* on your forehead?"

Bhimrao stops in his tracks. This well-born woman just called him brother. "First, my men must enter. Check for weapons and disarm everyone," he says gruffly.

"Of course."

Half a dozen men — led by Mahadev, the gang's second-in-command — slip indoors and come back carrying small kitchen knives and gardening and farming implements, which they stack on the veranda. Bhimrao looks inquiringly at Mahadev.

"Everything seems okay, but I think there's a plot," says Mahadev.

"May I please greet you formally now?" Parvati bai asks.

Bhimrao nods. He slings his rifle on his arm, indicating that the others should keep their guns ready. Stepping up, Parvati bai marks Bhimrao's sweaty forehead with vermillion paste. She puts a garland of marigolds around his neck and offers him a long, wide strip of white cloth, which is traditionally tied into a turban.

"Please come in." She leads them past an outer room into the inner courtyard. Rows of rugs have been laid down on the mud-packed floor. Banana leaves line the rugs, with aluminum and silver bowls and glasses set next to them. In the centre of the room, there are large cauldrons full of food.

"*Bhau*, I would like to serve you all a meal, just as I do with all the visitors who come to my house," says Parvati bai. She points at a bundle lying in the corner. "That is all the jewellery in the house. You may take whatever else you want, though I entreat you to let me keep my *mangalsutra*." Parvati bai fingers the beads of her necklace. "But first you must eat."

"You're going to poison us! Do you think we're fools?" Mahadev roars.

"You're my guests. If I hurt even a hair on your head, I will accumulate a lot of bad karma," says Parvati bai. "The first person to eat the food will be our servant, Ganpat. He will be served from the same pots that you see here. I could go first to prove that the food is fine, but the lady of the house must eat last. This is our custom."

Mahadev starts to speak again, but Bhimrao restrains him with an outstretched arm. A server brings a large plate of food to Ganpat, who sits cross-legged on the floor. Everyone watches as he somehow manages to gulp it all down, half choking, wishing he were dead. A few minutes pass.

"As you see, Ganpat is fine. He ate a little strangely, but that's because he is very scared," says Parvati bai.

PARVATI BAI AND THE BANDITS

Is this woman laughing at us? Bhimrao wonders. The aromas permeating the courtyard overpower him, and he asks all but four of his men to take a seat. "They'll eat later. They must guard us," he says.

Parvati bai nods, signalling the maids to start serving the best, most delicious, most memorable meal Bhimrao and his *toli* will ever eat.

There are crispy sabudana wadas, savoury tapioca fritters with flecks of green chili; masale bhaat, a delicious combo of rice, vegetables, and a special spice mix called goda masala, all cooked in ghee; and amti, a pleasingly spiced dal, which has coconut flakes and kokam, a sour berry, among other seasonings. A mixed vegetable rassa, a gravy dish spiced yet again with the delightful goda masala, is also served.

The cooks have made zunka bhakar, typical farmer's fare. The zunka is made with chickpea flour and spices, including lots of fiery red chilies. It perfectly complements the bhakar, made with pearl millet flour and accompanied by a dollop of freshly churned white butter. And there are chutneys and salads. Flax seed, coconut-garlic, and peanut chutneys. Two salads — one raw, one cooked — the former made with cooling cucumber and the latter with steamed pumpkin and homemade yogurt. There are also glasses of frothy buttermilk flavoured with asafoetida and cumin.

Parvati bai has not stinted on dessert. There is sweet and tart shrikhand, flecked with strands of saffron, the king of spices. Also karanji, a deep-fried pastry stuffed with sweetened coconut flavoured with nutmeg, and the dessert considered the greatest of them all — puran poli. This soft, thinly layered flatbread with a lentil and jaggery filling is aromatized with cardamom, the queen of spices.

The meal is entirely vegetarian, this being a Brahmin household.

The bandits eat with gusto. When their plates begin to empty, Parvati bai directs them to be filled up again. Bhimrao, always taciturn, eats in silence. A low-caste, illiterate man, he has followed his uncle into the profession. We will never know his thoughts, but a couple of times a smile lights up his stern face and reaches his eyes.

"What a grand feast, and all wasted on *dakus*. Can you imagine?" the head cook whispers to one of the maids. The maid moves away, carrying in a tray of paan. Each digestive is a beautiful, dark green triangle made with betel leaves and stuffed with goodies. A single clove holds the folds together.

When they are finally done eating, Mahadev wants to take the jewellery, as well as the silverware. "Let's go to the stable and take a few horses, too, if they're any good," he says.

Bhimrao holds up his hand, requesting silence. Then he says, "Sister, we'll leave now. We'll not take anything, because you have shown us such respect. Some of our men are not here. We split up into two groups. One group was sent to find, disarm, and tie up the men who would try to defend the village. We will go now and tell our comrades to release them. Your husband will return home safe. Thank you."

PARVATI BAI AND THE BANDITS

Bhimrao folds his hands in a namaste and bows his head. Parvati bai follows suit. In that moment she feels that Bhimrao really is her brother, a brother for whom she has questions. Who is he, really? What made him take this path? She feels the tight fist of tension in her gut beginning to loosen as a wave of fatigue hits her. She steadies herself with effort.

After the bandits leave, Parvati bai thanks all the servants and asks them to eat. She goes into the back room where Lali sits, her head nodding, half asleep. Parvati bai collapses against the girl, who wakes with a start, and holds her. Reverentially, they stand before a shrine, hands folded. Inside is a black stone idol of Jagdamba, their clan goddess, clad in an orange saree with a golden border, bedecked with flowers. She looks eerily real and has large resplendent eyes, and while her face is well carved, the rest of her is a block of polished black stone. In front of the goddess is a silver plate heaped with food — a ritual offering. "You must eat from that blessed plate now. I will wait for Sawant Rao," says Parvati bai.

"I feel like I'm in a dream. I can't believe it's over and we're all safe. Nothing was stolen. All because of you!" Lali looks admiringly at Parvati bai.

"It was such a gamble. I had no idea if it would work. I was very tense all night," says Parvati bai simply.

Bhimrao never enters Parvati bai's village again, and he issues a warning to other outlaws not to harm his sister and her family in any way. Every year during the Rakhi festival, when a sister ties an amulet around her brother's wrist to proclaim their protective bond, Bhimrao's face emerges in Parvati bai's consciousness — the hooded eyes, the dark skin, the oversized moustache, and the ugly scar that is almost a gash on his cheek. He remembers her too. They look at each other, holding their gaze for a long time.

PARVATI BAI'S RASSA

A mixed vegetable curry with goda masala from Maharashtra

Vegan, gluten-free, contains nuts
Servings: 4 | Cook Time: 1 hour, approximately |
Level: Medium

INGREDIENTS

- 3 heaped cups of mixed vegetables (potatoes, green peas, green beans, carrots, etc.), chopped
- 2 tablespoons cooking oil
- ½ teaspoon cumin seeds
- ½ teaspoon black mustard seeds
- ¼ teaspoon turmeric powder
- 2 pinches of asafoetida
- 8 fresh curry leaves (optional)
- 1 medium onion, cut into ½-inch pieces
- ½ teaspoon salt (to taste)

½ tablespoon grated ginger (or ready-made paste)

½ tablespoon minced garlic (or ready-made paste)

¼ cup desiccated unsweetened coconut (or frozen coconut, defrosted)

1 cup water, approximately

4 tablespoons roasted peanuts or raw cashews

2 teaspoons goda masala (to taste) (recipe on pages 35-36)

¼ teaspoon red chili powder (to taste)

⅛ teaspoon sugar

½ cup fresh tomatoes, diced (or canned tomatoes, chopped)

For the garnish:

4 tablespoons fresh cilantro, finely chopped

METHOD

1. Dense vegetables, like potatoes and carrots, should be parboiled to reduce the time needed to cook in the gravy.

2. Heat the oil in a thick-bottomed pot on high heat. Add cumin seeds, mustard seeds, turmeric powder, and asafoetida. When the seed spices (mustard and cumin) start sizzling, reduce heat and add the onion and salt. Fry well, adding a little water (2-3 tablespoons) if the mixture starts sticking to the bottom. Add curry leaves and fry for 1 minute.

3. Add ginger and garlic and fry until mixture becomes fragrant. Add coconut and fry for 2-3 minutes until the coconut releases an aroma and turns slightly darker. Take care not to burn the coconut.

4. Add all the vegetables. Reduce heat and fry for 1 minute. Add the water, nuts, goda masala, chili powder, and sugar. After the first 5 minutes of cooking, add the tomatoes. Cover and cook on medium heat until vegetables are just cooked (al dente), stirring occasionally. Once the vegetables are done, reduce heat to minimum and simmer for 10 minutes.
5. Remove from heat. Taste and adjust the spices. You can add more chili, goda masala, and salt, but not the spices that were fried.
6. Serve hot, garnished with the fresh cilantro. Serve on rice or with Indian bread or Greek pita. Sides include natural yogurt, chutneys, pickles, salads, and papadum.

NOTES

1. Indian cooking needs a cooking oil with a high-smoke point, such as sunflower, vegetable, or canola oil.
2. Asafoetida can be bought whole in some natural food stores or online, then crushed into a powder. It can also be bought as a powder at Indian stores, but often contains additives, including wheat. Be sure to look for a gluten-free version if there are allergy concerns.
3. Buy fresh curry leaves in an Indian shop. Remove stems and freeze leaves in an airtight container. Defrost before using.
4. Try to get Indian red chili powder from an Indian shop. It's a good idea to taste the raw red chili

powder to determine the taste and heat, as it will be new to many. If you need to substitute, use cayenne pepper powder.

GODA MASALA

A flavourful regional spice mix

Making a spice mix (masala) from scratch is fun and easy. You can sprinkle this yummy masala on salads and use it to pep up any savoury dish. Use it in vegetable, lentil, rice dishes, etc., just like other spice mixes, such as garam masala and curry powder.

Vegan, gluten-free
Yield: 1 cup | Cook time: 15 minutes |
Level: Easy

INGREDIENTS
Spices to dry roast:

- 6 tablespoons coriander seeds
- 6 tablespoons white sesame seeds
- 1 tablespoon cumin seeds
- 1½ scant teaspoons peppercorns
- 1 scant teaspoon cloves
- 2 bay leaves
- 1 cinnamon stick, 1 inch long

Spices to add after grinding:

¼ teaspoon asafoetida

½ teaspoon turmeric

METHOD

1. In a bowl, mix all of the spices to dry roast.
2. Heat a non-stick pan on medium. When the pan is moderately hot, spread the spices evenly on it.
3. The spices will darken and start releasing an aroma after about 2–3 minutes. Exact timing depends on a number of factors, so go by look and smell, not by time.
4. Transfer the spices to a plate and let cool. Then grind them to a fine powder in a good-quality food processor or spice grinder.
5. Transfer the spice powder back to the bowl, add the remaining ingredients, and mix well. Transfer to an airtight container.

NOTES

1. Reduce the amount of cloves and peppercorns if you can't tolerate heat.
2. Asafoetida can be bought whole in some natural food stores or online, then crushed into a powder. It can also be bought as a powder at Indian stores, but often contains additives, including wheat. Be sure to look for a gluten-free version if there are allergy concerns.
3. Goda masala can be stored in a dark place for up to 6 months and in the fridge for an additional 6 months.

THE EMPEROR WHO LOVED MANGOES

Characters
Akbar, a Moghul emperor
Birbal, a Hindu courtier and advisor
Javed and Maaz, two farmers
Shamu, a day labourer

That evening, Emperor Akbar was taking his customary stroll through his beautifully laid-out garden, accompanied by his advisor and friend, Birbal. "I have a little puzzle for you," said Akbar.

"At your service, *Jahan Panha*, 'One Who Provides Shelter to the World,'" Birbal responded.

"Why such formality? I suppose you're laughing at me?" Akbar was referring to the honorific Birbal had used.

"*Tauba, tauba* ... I repent. Do you doubt my sincerity?" asked Birbal in mock outrage.

Shrugging, Akbar started recounting what had transpired that morning. Having woken up as usual, a little before dawn, he dressed and prayed to Allah, facing west, looking toward Mecca. Then he proceeded to the *jharokha darshan*, the ornate balcony from where he greeted the sun every morning. Akbar had adopted the Hindu practice of saluting the sun as it rose, viewing it from the balcony. A crowd of his subjects — soldiers, small traders, craftsmen, peasants, and women bearing sick children in their arms — stood below, saluting both the emperor and the sun and praying. The women believed that a glimpse of the emperor could cure their children.

On this public balcony, Akbar did not allow his courtiers to introduce him with pomp and ceremony, rattling off a list of honorifics as was customary. Nor did they announce him by his full name: Abu'l-Fath Jalal ud-Din Muhammad Akbar. Rather, he was just like the others, partaking in a sacred ritual. He wished to be accessible to his people and to start his day with them. Later, he held court on the same spot, with people presenting their problems and complaints directly to him.

That day, two men fell to fighting in the crowd. They had to be separated by the sentries and were about to be taken to the gates of the Agra Fort, the emperor's residence, when Akbar intervened. He asked that they be presented to him later that morning in the *Diwan-i-Am*, a pillared hall where he met commoners. A couple of hours later, Javed and Maaz, the farmers who had been caught fighting, were brought before the emperor. Looking sheepish, they bowed low, then prostrated before him. Akbar was surprised to see that both were well into their fifties. He had expected younger men, immature, quick to anger. "It was rather lively, the fight this morning. We rarely have such spontaneous scenes here," said Akbar.

"*Jahan Panha, mafi, mafi.* Forgive us," said Javed, falling to his knees again. He was slim and good-looking, with a well-trimmed beard, while Maaz was stout, plain, and clean-shaven.

Akbar gestured that Javed should rise. "So, what brought on the fight? Perhaps I could help."

"Oh, no, no, it's nothing. We don't want to bother you. If I had known that Javed would be here this morning, I would not have come at all," said Maaz.

"Why so? Is he your enemy?" Akbar asked.

Lowering his gaze, Maaz said nothing.

"Your lordship, our farms are right next to each other. The problem is that Maaz is making claims on my mango tree and that has divided us," said Javed.

Akbar leaned forward. "What kind of mango tree is it?"

"Totapuri," Maaz responded.

"Why, that is among my favourites! Totapuri — a prince of mangoes. It is one of the varieties that I have planted in Lakhi Bagh. You know that over one hundred thousand mango trees grow there, and the diversity is quite astounding."

"Yes, sire. We have heard about your wonderful orchard," said Javed.

Akbar continued, "Not a single fruit did my father and grandfather find pleasing in Hindustan when they came here. How could they ever forget the divine taste of Persian melons and the sweetness of apples from Samarkand? I am indebted to them for introducing exotic fruits here. I, too, have contributed by setting up my imperial fruitery and bringing over horticulturists from Persia and central Asia. Fruits are the greatest gift the creator has bequeathed on his creatures. What do you say to that?"

Maaz and Javed nodded, a little uneasy. They had not expected such an informal exchange with the One Who Provides Shelter to the World.

"But there is one and only one fruit in India that rivals those from my ancestral homelands," Akbar continued. "It is of course the mango. A royal fruit, fit for a great court."

The courtier, who stood fidgeting a little behind Akbar, cleared his throat. There were people waiting for the emperor, important people.

"Whose mango tree is it, then? Surely, that is well known!" said Akbar.

"Mine," said Javed and Maaz at the same time. They both glared at each other.

"Peace. I will put the question to Birbal this very evening," said Akbar.

The men nodded.

After recounting the story of the fight between Javed and Maaz to Birbal in the royal gardens, Akbar continued: "These peasants don't live very far, just on the outskirts of Agra. I have told them that I will send for them as soon as you have an answer."

"I think I will make a little trip to their village. I've an idea I want to pursue," said Birbal.

"Splendid."

They walked on in silence for a few minutes.

"All this talk of mangoes brought to mind how you humiliated me before Mariam-uz-Zamani," Akbar said.

Birbal warmed to the subject. He liked Mariam-uz-Zamani, one of Akbar's chief queens. She was a Hindu Rajput princess from the kingdom of Amber. Though the alliance was forged for political reasons, she had gained status in the harem of her own accord.

"It was not my intent, *Shahenshah*, King of Kings, to humiliate you in any way. I merely wanted to defend the queen. I recall that you were sitting right here in this garden with her. You were both eating mangoes with great relish. While there was a pile of mango skins and mango seeds near the queen, there was nothing near you," said Birbal.

"Because I had put my skins and seeds in her pile."

"You said, 'Look Birbal, look at Mariam-uz-Zamani's greed. She has eaten all those mangoes by herself, while I have eaten none.'"

"To which, Birbal, you responded, 'Nay, you have eaten not just the flesh of the mangoes, but the skins and seeds as well. Who then would you say is the greedier of the two?'"

"And was that unjust?"

"Not at all. You just caught me out, as usual."

"The queen was most gracious in inviting my family to dinner. How wonderful they were, those dishes from her homeland! Dal-bati-churma, gatte ka saag, ker sangri, imarti. My mouth waters as I recall that meal."

"It was indeed memorable. And all vegetarian, given Mariam's beliefs and your own."

"We ate panchmel dal for the first time, and my wife now uses the queen's recipe to make it at home."

"I like it as well, simple though it is. It is interesting, Birbal, to observe how new habits form and novel preferences develop. I abstained from meat three times a week, even before I married Mariam. The vegetarian dishes she introduced into the royal kitchen made that custom easier. I used to fast before our marriage, too, and now I fast a bit more, following her example. It is good for body and soul. However, there is another problem that I would like to bring to you."

Stopping at a beautiful rose bush, Akbar bent down and lustily inhaled the fragrance of a particularly spectacular flower. "The queen has proved to be insatiable. She may not have eaten the most mangoes, but she keeps trying to get me to renounce meat altogether. You know that I'm not that fond of meat, but I must eat some. Otherwise, it would be disrespectful to my family, my heritage, and my courtiers."

"That is indeed a dilemma, sire. Perhaps you need to distract Mariam-uz-Zamani from these concerns. You do praise her, I believe, for all the good things that she has brought to the court? How she suggested that you open your mind to other religions and new ideas? That you learn more about them? And this you have done admirably."

"Any praise from you is high praise, Birbal. I would greatly appreciate it if you had a private audience with Mariam and explained my situation. She holds you in high esteem, and you have a way with words."

Birbal bowed. Soon he took his leave and made his way home. *How stimulating it is to converse with the emperor,* he thought. Participating in all this invigorating activity that takes place around him makes it easier to ignore the barbs from some of the orthodox Muslim courtiers. Birbal was one of the *navratanas*, or the nine jewels, in Akbar's court. These nine outstanding men, skilled in various ways, were integral to court life. Inevitably, some of the courtiers were jealous of their special status.

Two days after his conversation with Akbar, Birbal raised some dust as he rode swiftly to the village where the two farmers lived. A courtier followed him on another fine horse. Just as they reached the village, a fiery crimson ball rose majestically over the wheat fields, outlining the silhouettes of the trees that dotted them. They reined in their horses and paused to admire nature's handiwork. Birbal sighed, wishing that he could escape from the Agra Fort more often.

Word about his impending visit was sent to the farmers, with instructions to keep it quiet, but the arrival of two strangers on thoroughbred horses brought people out of their homes.

Soon Birbal was admiring a wonderful mango tree — tall and healthy, densely leafed, though bereft of blossoms, as they were in the middle of a cold northern winter. Standing under the rounded canopy of the tree with Javed and Maaz, he inhaled deeply the delightful fragrance of mango leaves. "How many mangoes did you get last year?" he asked.

"About two hundred. This tree is nearly eleven years old," said Maaz.

"Yes, I'd say two hundred," agreed Javed.

"Let's sit comfortably and talk," Birbal said.

He was given a seat on an upturned wooden box on which Maaz had spread a thick wool blanket, apologizing repeatedly for his humble circumstances. His wife, her face veiled, served Birbal and his companion cups of steaming, milky, sugary tea. The two farmers sat down on the ground before them.

"I sent a couple of men to the village yesterday to ask the villagers whom they thought the mango tree belonged to. Perhaps because you live beyond the creek and your lands are at some distance from the village, or perhaps for other reasons, there was no consensus among the villagers about the ownership of the tree," said Birbal. "Given the situation, I propose the following: together, you must cut the tree down and divide the wood between you."

No sooner had the words left his lips than a sound like that of a wounded animal escaped Maaz. "No, that's out of the question!" he said.

"But that's a good idea," said Javed.

"I see no other way. Believe me, I have thought deeply," said Birbal.

Clasping his hands together, with tears in his voice and eyes, Maaz said, "Sire, I have raised the tree with as much care as my children, even more care, I would say. I truly love it. I will not cut it down. Let Javed have it. Let him harvest and take all the fruit. But I will lay down one condition. He must look after it well, so that it continues to grow and remains healthy and happy."

"Clearly, the tree belongs to Maaz, who has lovingly tended it for over a decade. According to royal decree, the tree will remain with Maaz. It will be passed down to future generations. As for Javed, he must pay a fine for attempted theft," Birbal said gravely.

"But sir ..." Javed started to say.

Birbal silenced him with an upraised hand.

"You must come again during the harvest. Nay, I will bring a basket of the best totapuri mangoes to you," Maaz said joyfully.

"That is an offer hard to refuse," said Birbal with a smile. He turned to Javed. "Tell me, Javed, why did you make a claim on the tree? You've been neighbours with Maaz for a long time. Am I right?"

"Our families have lived here, side by side, for generations," said Maaz.

Javed hesitated, then said, "As the tree grew, it cast a large shadow on my land. Nothing grows well under its shade."

Maaz looked surprised. "I had not thought of that!" he exclaimed. "Why then, Javed need not pay a fine. And I pledge to give some mangoes to him every year."

Birbal soon took his leave and headed back home, the courtier riding a few paces behind.

Near Agra Fort was a small lake. As they approached the lake, Birbal saw that four palace guards were waiting on the shore. When he spotted the emperor, Birbal stopped and dismounted.

"I decided to come and meet you here. I'm keen to know what transpired," said Akbar, smiling. After he heard the story, the emperor was full of praise for Birbal. "I look forward to some of those totapuri mangoes," he added.

"But you get such choice fruit from your own orchards!" said Birbal.

"My workers look after hundreds of trees. They are hired labour, while Maaz tends this one tree so lovingly. I expect superior results, don't you?"

"I will send some over," said Birbal, a hint of merriment in his voice.

The emperor's extreme love for fruit always amused Birbal. It seemed that they were more precious to him than gems.

"My summers would be terrible if I could not swim in lakes such as this one. The summers here are so scorching," said Akbar as they made their way toward the horses.

"I wonder how cold the water is now," said Birbal.

"You could find out for yourself."

"I prefer to remain ignorant, my lord. I can bet you, though, that a very poor man will agree to spend a night standing in that water for a large sum of money."

"Impossible!"

Birbal forgot his remark, but Akbar did not. Soon an announcement was made throughout the kingdom that a man who would spend all night standing waist-deep in a cold lake would get fifty gold coins. The emperor was taken aback to hear that a line of men had formed at the entrance of the fort on the appointed day. It was only fair to pick the first one who had arrived — an emaciated day labourer named Shamu, who had nine daughters but not a single one wedded because he could not afford any dowry for them.

News about this strange challenge spread rapidly through the kingdom, and people started taking bets on whether the man would stay the course or quit halfway. That evening, Shamu was taken to the lake, and two guards were posted to keep an eye on him. Early the next morning,

Shamu was brought to Akbar, having stood waist-deep in the water, not far from the shore, all night. Akbar sent him off for a warm bath and a sumptuous breakfast before meeting him again in the *Diwan-i-Khas*, a pillared hall, where some courtiers were seated. A commoner never entered this precinct, but Shamu was an exception.

"How did you do it? Tell me your secret," said Akbar.

At first Shamu said nothing and stood with his head bowed. Much cajoling brought out this account in fits and starts. "*Jahan Panha*, there is a street lamp some distance away. When I was going to give up after two hours in the freezing water, I saw the street light and I thought, let me imagine the warmth of that lamp. Let me imagine the heat of a fire. The warmth gave me hope that I can marry my daughters off honourably and build a proper house for my wife. But if I had to do it again, I would say no, for it was very difficult."

On hearing this, one of the courtiers, a proud man of high rank, said, "This man has cheated, sire! He has warmed himself by the heat of a street light. He has therefore lost the wager. He should not be paid a *paisa*."

The other courtiers also had things to say, and a heated debate ensued. Shamu stood shaking a little, his heart quaking. Finally, Akbar told him that the matter needed to be considered further. He asked a courtier to get the man's address, and Shamu left the fort, wretched. Gamblers around the country were thrown into a quandary. Those who had betted on the man staying in the lake all night claimed that

THE EMPEROR WHO LOVED MANGOES

they had won, but their opponents believed the opposite. Many heated words were exchanged, and a couple of men even came to blows, but no money exchanged hands.

That night, Akbar went to bed disturbed. He was also a little angry with Birbal for coming up with the idea in the first place. And instead of helping him deal with the situation, Birbal had not come to court all day. The next morning there was important business at hand, and all the courtiers had been asked to come early to the *Diwan-i-Khas*. Everyone obliged, but there was no sign of Birbal. Akbar sent a couple of men to Birbal's house to find out if he was ill. They returned and reported that he was fine but occupied with something important. Irritated, Akbar continued with the business of the day, and the day passed without Birbal appearing.

That evening, Akbar went to Birbal's house. He walked directly into the inner courtyard to find Birbal sitting by a small collection of nearly burnt-out twigs. High above was a brass pot suspended on a makeshift wooden frame. "Birbal! What are you up to?" the emperor exclaimed.

Birbal stood up and bowed respectfully. "I am making khichari, my lord."

"But how absurd! How can you expect that little fire, which isn't even a fire really, to cook the rice and lentils in that pot high above?"

"If a man can get warmth from a distant street lamp as he stands in a freezing lake, surely my khichari, too, will feel the heat from the fire and cook."

The emperor burst out laughing. "I will send for Shamu first thing tomorrow, and not only will I give him more than the promised reward, but I will also confer on him a title that is reserved for bravery in battle."

"That would be justice done."

"You have inadvertently proven, Birbal, that hope is the greatest beacon."

"Well said, Emperor."

"And how did you come upon this stratagem to convince me?"

"Actually, the idea came up during a discussion with my wife," Birbal admitted.

"I see. I may also send a little recompense your way."

Just then, Birbal's vivacious young daughter, who had been skipping rope in a corner of the courtyard, came up to them. Bowing low to Akbar, she said, "*Jahan Panha*, just in case the reward is in gold coins, they will go from my father directly to my mother, then straight into the safe, where she is accumulating money for my dowry." With these words, she skipped out of the courtyard, giggling.

"Brazen girl," said Birbal, shaking his head. "Don't mind her. Hard to keep in check."

"As the tree, so shall be the fruit," said Akbar.

The emperor looked triumphant, while Birbal looked a little embarrassed.

MANGO LASSI AKBARI

A mango-flavoured yogurt drink — a royal treat

Vegetarian, gluten-free, contains nuts
Servings: 2–4 | Prep Time: 10 minutes | Level: Easy

INGREDIENTS

- 1 cup ripe mango pieces, skin removed (or frozen mango, defrosted)
- 1 cup natural yogurt (2% or richer)
- 1 cup milk (2% or richer)
- 2 tablespoons sugar (to taste)
- ¼ teaspoon cardamom powder (to taste)
- 1 teaspoon rosewater
- 4 tablespoons pistachios or almonds, coarsely powdered

METHOD

1. Blend mango, yogurt, milk, sugar, cardamom, and rosewater in a food processor or blender. Add half the powdered pistachios or almonds. Pour into glasses.

2. Add ice cubes and garnish with the remaining powdered nuts. If you wish, you can add a dash of cardamom powder before serving.

NOTE
1. How much sugar you use depends on the sweetness of the mango and the sourness of the yogurt. Taste both the mango and yogurt before deciding on the amount of sugar. You can also make this recipe without sugar.

THREE GRAINS OF MUSTARD

Characters
Kisa Gotami, our heroine
Sanu, her son
Avni, her sister-in-law
Shalva, her father-in-law
Kosi, her husband
Siddhartha Gautama, the Buddha

A clear blue sky curved above a field of swaying golden wheat stalks. The sun warmed Kisa Gotami's back as she bent over the stalks, cutting them at their roots. A pile of wheat stalks lay in the little clearing Kisa Gotami had made in the field. The wind suddenly picked up and the sky darkened. Her head scarf was undone and whipped around her eyes, the scythe falling from her hand. The scarf wrapped itself around her neck, tight as a noose. Terrified, she struggled with it, managing to pull it off. Rubbing her neck, she looked up at the sky. Raindrops fat as fists were hurtling down, slapping her upturned face. Then she saw it. It was the scythe, coming at her through the air.

"Nahiiiiii!" she screamed, falling to the ground. The scythe landed on her thigh. A deep wound opened, and blood, black as night, roared out.

Hearing the scream from her room, Avni grabbed her candlestick and rushed to her sister-in-law's bedside. As Kisa Gotami awakened, her eyes rested on the fine mesh of the mosquito net that encased the four-poster bed on which she lay. Her son, Sanu, was asleep beside her, breathing noisily. "*Bhabhi* ... sister-in-law," said Avni softly.

Kisa Gotami turned and saw Avni, who had set down the candlestick and was offering her a glass of water. Parting the folds of the mosquito net, she gratefully accepted the drink. She was sweating, and her heartbeat had not yet returned to normal. "Kosi was just here. He asked, 'Where is Sanu, my son?'" she whispered.

THREE GRAINS OF MUSTARD

Avni looked at Kisa Gotami, her eyes wide with concern. It had been a year since Avni's brother Kosi had passed away. The family had recently held a ceremony to commemorate the anniversary of his death. The *vaidya* had come two days earlier and prescribed some medicines for Sanu's fever. But it had not abated, continuing to fluctuate. Even Kisa Gotami's ailing father-in-law, Shalva, who rarely left his room, had come to see Sanu.

Tears filled Kisa Gotami's eyes, and she clung to Avni's arm. After a few moments, Kisa Gotami said, "I must get the lemongrass for the tea."

"Please rest some more," said Avni.

Not wanting to displease her, Kisa Gotami lay back in bed. She felt weak. She had lost her appetite since Sanu had taken ill. She turned toward her son. Softly, she kissed his forehead, breathing in his smell. Mixed in with sweat and the sweet smell of his body, there were other odours — unknown, unpleasant. All the same, she felt a little reassured. *I will not stay in bed for long*, she told herself. Instead, she fell asleep.

Two hours later Kisa Gotami made her way to the woodlot that bordered the family estate. The thick pelt of grass under her bare feet was soft, warm, and pleasing, yet her mind raced. *Could God take my Sanu? He has already taken Kosi. Wasn't one death enough? Even if God gave that cruel command, Death would show mercy. Death would surely disobey.*

Catching sight of the trees, her mind began to quieten. Their branches were like arms extending outward; their foliage gave shelter to all. For a few moments, she stood still under a blossoming mango tree, inhaling the fragrance. Mango season would soon be in full swing.

She felt hopeful as she gathered some lemongrass and made a pouch with the end of her saree to hold it. She would boil it with ginger powder, pepper pods, and cinnamon sticks to make a potent tea. It was a remedy they used in her village, and she trusted it more than the powders that the city doctor had given, which had not worked. She would make the tea herself, even though her mother-in-law was not pleased when she went into the kitchen.

This was her real home, this woodlot where all the forces of nature came together to provide her with beauty and security. She came here often with Sanu. Even if he was cranky or restless, the place seemed to soothe him. He would quieten and gaze around him, his eyes wide with wonder. She felt like an outsider in that grand house where she lived, so different from the humble hut where she had grown up.

Five summers ago, Shalva had set up shop right in the middle of the bustling market. He drew attention, this man clad in fine clothes sitting on an ornate chair, a servant holding a decorated umbrella over his head to shield him from the sun.

THREE GRAINS OF MUSTARD 57

He did not look like any other seller in that busy market in the thriving city of Savatthi.

While his appearance drew looks and whispers, his goods made people stop and stare. Heaps of ashes, yes, that's what he was selling. Before long, news that a wealthy man was selling ashes went around the market, and throngs formed to see for themselves. People laughed at Shalva and called him a fool, but Shalva sat expressionless and silent.

A couple of days earlier, Shalva had paid his daily visit to his golden room. This was a small storeroom inside his large house, filled with gold bricks. The bricks were under lock and key, and the keys hung on a gold chain around his neck. Admiring his wealth every single day gave him great pleasure. But when he entered that morning, he saw that all the bricks had turned to ashes.

Shalva rushed out of the room, screaming, and ran into his friend who had come by for a cup of tea. When Shalva told him what had happened and how he was a ruined man, his friend said, "It's all very clear, my dear man. Your money was just sitting in that room in the form of gold. It was not being used. It was therefore worthless. And so it has turned into ashes."

Shalva stared at his friend. "But what can I do now?"

"Calm down first. Let me think."

Shalva waited eagerly. His friend had a reputation as a wise man. Shalva called a servant, asking him to bring hot tea and some snacks. The tea arrived, and after a few sips, his friend said, "Well, it seems to me that you should sell the ashes at the market. This is what you have now — ashes, not gold. Who knows what may transpire as a result?"

The desperate man followed his friend's advice. And there he was, having made no sales all day, being derided by people far beneath him. He was about to pack up and go home when Kisa Gotami came by. Born into a low-caste family that lived on the outskirts of Savatthi, she had come to deliver a message from her father to her uncle. Her uncle had a small stall in the market, and she was now on her way home. As she paused at Shalva's stall, she heard him offer a passerby a *seer* of ashes for a very low price. When the would-be customer shook his head, Shalva lowered the price. The man shook his head again and went on his way.

"Sir, why are you selling gold so cheaply?" asked Kisa Gotami. Her plain, pleasant face reflected astonishment. With these words, she picked up some ashes in her cupped palm, and they turned into gleaming gold nuggets. Shalva could not believe his eyes. He eagerly asked her to touch all the piles, and they all turned into gold. Immensely relieved, he gave Kisa Gotami his address and told her to come over the next day for her reward.

"Why a reward, sir?"

Shalva merely insisted and then told a servant to get her whereabouts in case she failed to show up.

Back home, Shalva told his friend everything.

"That is a special person, a very special person indeed," said the friend.

"Yes, she performed a miracle."

"It's not that. She's spiritual and sees things for what they really are, not what they seem to be."

"I see," said Shalva thoughtfully. "She deserves a great reward. But I cannot decide how much gold she should have."

"Is she married or single?"

"Why? I mean, I don't know. She is of marriageable age, but she did not have any of the marks of a married woman."

"Why give her gold then? Give her a worthy husband. Perhaps your eldest son? I think that would be a fitting reward. And she would be a valuable addition to the family, don't you think?"

A poor, dark-skinned woman, thin as a stick but strong, entered a rich man's house as a new bride. Is it difficult to imagine what happened next?

Most of the family members snubbed her. A few merely tolerated her. The rejection did not wipe the ready smile off Kisa Gotami's lips, nor did it change her helpful nature. She learned fast and worked hard, winning over a few. Husband and wife bonded in quiet affection and became devoted to each other.

Three years passed, yet Kisa Gotami had not conceived, much to the displeasure of her in-laws. She always offered alms to every holy man who came to their door. Holy man or beggar, she never turned anyone away. She started asking the holy men for help. In any case, there was no shortage of remedies for barren women. Advice came at her from every quarter. She had nothing to lose, so she tried all the remedies. At last, one day, she became pregnant. It was a difficult pregnancy, and the birth was no easier. The child, Sanu, became the centre of her world. She was simply the happiest, most loving mother of them all.

One day Kosi was thrown off a horse. He broke his back and slowly wasted away over many months. Sanu was a frail one-year-old when he lost his father. Since widows were responsible for the death of their husbands, Kisa Gotami had not only killed Kosi, but as a widow, she was also sure to bring more misfortune to the family. The family wanted to send her back to her parents' home and keep the boy with them. Though he was aging fast, Shalva still yielded some power. Kisa Gotami was not going anywhere, he declared. And so she remained, wearing the white clothes of a widow, receiving frugal meals. She shaved off her hair, but it grew back quickly. She draped the long end of her saree over her head to hide it. Since her shadow was unclean, polluting, she was mostly confined to her room.

Then Sanu became gravely ill, and for the first time, the family members found common ground as they rallied around him. As he got better and then got worse, Kisa Gotami's agitated mind flew between hope and fear, then back again. Avni, grounded in hope, became her beacon.

It was Avni, sleeping with Kisa Gotami and Sanu the night her nephew died, who discovered that the child had no pulse. Her quiet sobs had broken through Kisa Gotami's troubled dreams. Death unhinged the mother. Death, with whom she had pleaded, over and over again, to bypass her child. She refused to accept that Sanu was dead and wandered the streets for hours, holding the child in her arms, asking for medicine for her boy. Her hair hung loose and dishevelled, framing her frantic face. Her eyes were wild. Her saree was crumpled and ripped in a couple of places.

"Please, sir," she said to the men who passed her. "My boy is very ill. He needs medicine. Can you please help? Can you please find some medicine for him?"

At first people interacted with her, but they soon realized that the poor child had passed away. She shook her head, her desperation growing when people stopped responding to her cries, when they started turning away when she approached them. Then she remembered the temple priest who had come to the house to perform a *puja*, which she had watched from a distance. He was very learned and wise, like the holy men who had helped her conceive. The priest would surely have medicine for her boy.

At the temple the priest towered above her, God-like. He wore a crisp and spotless white *dhoti*. His bare chest was encircled by a thread that declared his status as a Brahmin, twice born. His broad forehead was marked with white lines.

Little gold loops decorated his earlobes. His head was almost bald, with only a tuft of hair left at the back.

How regal he is, she thought. *Close to God.* Appealing to Death had not worked, so now she directed her faith toward God and the priest.

"I cannot help you, Kisa Gotami," said the priest. She stared at him, stunned. "But there is someone who may be able to help."

Siddhartha Gautama was sitting under a tree, surrounded by a crowd. His reputation had sprouted and spread in just a few years. He had drawn followers from the princely class, to which he had belonged, and Brahmins into his fold. Merchants followed his teachings, too, as did the lowliest of men in the caste hierarchy. Women were also drawn to his ideas. High-caste women, led by his adoptive mother, wanted to enter the fold as *bhikkhunis,* Buddhist nuns, and to this Siddhartha Gautama had finally agreed.

Kisa Gotami fought her way through the crowd to get close to Siddhartha Gautama. She regarded the man, who was sermonizing. A strange aura defined him, strange and potent. She could not focus on his words, but she was mesmerized. Siddhartha Gautama was engrossed in his teaching, but he noticed the woman carrying a limp child in her arms. He paused and beckoned one of the disciples, asking him

THREE GRAINS OF MUSTARD 63

in an undertone to go speak to her. The man returned and whispered that the woman was mad. She had her dead child in her arms, but she refused to believe that he was lifeless.

"Let her approach," said Siddhartha Gautama.

Kisa Gotami eagerly stepped forward and told her story, asking for medicine, a remedy.

"You have done well to come here. I will help you. We will make a remedy for your son," he said.

Kisa Gotami smiled, a wave of relief rolling over her. She was heard! She was believed!

"I want you to go and fetch me three grains of mustard. They will go into the medicine I will make. Go to the nearest house and ask the woman there," he said.

"Yes, I will do so," she said joyfully.

"Leave the child here." Seeing her hesitate, he said, "He will be safe."

She believed him and her heart was full. Three grains of mustard! *This would be so easy to find*, she thought. *Everyone uses mustard to cook. The seeds are cheap and it is no luxury to give some away, and for such a good cause too. Soon Sanu would be well again. He would smile and gurgle and laugh.*

As Kisa Gotami turned to go, Siddhartha Gautama said, "There is one more thing. You must get the mustard seeds from a house that has not been touched by death. Make sure you ask the woman of the house if there has been a death in the family."

Kisa Gotami nodded. From door to door she went, asking for mustard seeds, saying that they were going to be used to make medicine for her sick child. Siddhartha Gautama had sent her, she explained. The women nodded and turned away to fetch her the grains.

"Has there been any death in your family? I must get the seeds from a house where there has been no death," Kisa Gotami said.

As soon as these words escaped her, everything changed. The women would stiffen, or their faces would soften and their eyes would become moist. A few burst into tears.

"My father-in-law passed away. It has been six months now ..."

"My uncle was suddenly taken ill ..."

"My dear little one, oh ... my lovely girl ..."

"It was my grandmother. She passed away in her sleep ..."

"Our cousin, he was sick for a long time ..."

Indefatigable, Kisa Gotami went from one house to the next, convinced that she would find the right house. All she needed was one. But as she heard tale after tale of death and loss, her heart began to open. Her vision, focused exclusively on Sanu, started expanding. She gradually awoke from her nightmare. She had lost touch with reason, taking refuge in the comforting idea that Sanu was merely ill. Reality was too terrifying; she did not know how to face it.

The dead weight that had pressed down on her soul started to shift. All beings will pass away one day, she realized. Numerous are the dead and few are the living. Kisa Gotami felt the pain of those who remained, those who were still

THREE GRAINS OF MUSTARD

alive. She wanted to help and learn from them and share her grief. She realized her connection to each and every one of them. All humans, all living creatures, are one family.

When she returned to the place where Siddhartha Gautama had been teaching, she found that the lay followers had dispersed, and he was now deep in discussion with some monks from his order. He noticed Kisa Gotami as she approached. "Did you find the mustard seeds?" he asked.

"I did not. I have come to bury my child," she said simply.

Two hours later a handful of the disciples and *bhikkhus*, Buddhist monks, and some women from the village accompanied her to the nearby forest. There she laid her child in a grave dug among ancient trees, where rays of sunlight filtered through the canopy of leaves and spread amid wildflowers, shrubs, and lichen. The forest reminded Kisa Gotami of the woodlot near her husband's home. After her son was buried, she looked up at everyone and said, "My Sanu will embark on the journey beyond this life. My duty as a mother is done."

One of the disciples spoke. "Siddhartha Gautama has taught us that change is a constant, the only constant. It is essential to accept the profound reality that nothing will be, can be, forever. How long does a flower live? Just a few days after appearing as a bud, it falls off the stem. We humans have difficulty accepting the inevitability of old age, sickness, and death. Attachment to the notion of permanence, in any shape or form, can only cause great suffering."

Kisa Gotami nodded. She was at peace, even as waves of grief washed over her. Difficult as it was to accept impermanence — the death of Sanu, the death of Kosi — she could see that there was no alternative. In a world where everything changes constantly, there is some serenity in accepting the truth that all phenomena are impermanent.

When Kisa Gotami returned to Siddhartha Gautama, she said, "I would like to become your disciple and join the order of *bhikkhunis*."

And to this he agreed.

CARROT-RADISH SALAD

A mustardy side dish from western India

Vegan, gluten-free, contains nuts
Servings: 4-6 | Cook Time: 15 minutes | Level: Easy

INGREDIENTS

- 1 cup carrot, grated
- 1 cup radish, grated
- 1 tablespoon lemon or lime juice (to taste)
- 2 tablespoons roasted peanuts (optional)
- ¼ teaspoon coriander powder
- ¼ teaspoon cumin powder
- ¼ teaspoon red chili powder (to taste)
- ⅛ teaspoon sugar

Spices to fry:

- 2 tablespoons cooking oil
- ½ teaspoon black mustard seeds
- ¼ teaspoon turmeric powder
- 2 pinches of asafoetida

For the garnish:

4 tablespoons fresh cilantro, finely chopped
¼ teaspoon salt (to taste)

METHOD

1. Place the grated carrot and radish in a serving dish. Mix in the lemon or lime juice, peanuts (if using), coriander powder, cumin powder, red chili powder, and sugar. Set aside.
2. In a small thick-bottomed pot, heat oil on high and add mustard seeds, turmeric powder, and asafoetida. When the mustard seeds start sizzling well, remove from heat and add fried spices to the carrot-radish mixture. Put some of the vegetable mixture back in the pot to scoop up all the fried spices. Return it to the serving dish and mix well. Taste and adjust spices.
3. Garnish with the chopped cilantro. Serve at room temperature or after being cooled in the fridge.
4. Add the salt just before serving.

NOTES

1. Indian cooking needs a cooking oil with a high-smoke point, such as sunflower, vegetable, or canola oil.
2. Asafoetida can be bought whole in some natural food stores or online, then crushed into a powder. It can also be bought as a powder at Indian stores, but often contains additives, including wheat. Be sure to look for a gluten-free version if there are allergy concerns.

ANNAPURNA'S SOUP KITCHEN

Characters
Parvati, a Hindu goddess
Shiva and Vishnu, Hindu gods
Indra, God of gods
Narada, a mythical Hindu sage
Amy, a university professor
Madan, her husband
Tara, her daughter

"Tell me story." Tara stood at the door of the study, holding a book. Pigtails framed her oval face. She had large dark eyes and skinny forearms.

Amy looked up from the paper she was marking. Essays were scattered all around her. A couple had fallen off the table and were lying on the intricately patterned wine-red carpet. She was only halfway through marking, and the papers were due the next morning.

"Later," she said.

"No!"

Tara's bedtime was creeping up, and Amy had refused her twice already. *When will she start reading?* Amy thought.

"Annapurna again?" Amy drawled.

Tara nodded, clutching the book to her chest as if it was Chuck, her stuffed rabbit. Amy got up from her desk, sighing, and moved to the sofa. Tara cuddled up beside her, smiling.

Amy considered the kitschy book cover.

There she was — Annapurna — a graceful, bejewelled woman with long, dark, and lustrous hair, wearing a red saree with a gold border, standing by a pot of yellowish porridge or something, and holding a ladle. Shiva stood beside her, holding a begging bowl. Both Parvati and Shiva, Shiva and Parvati, were smiling.

Shiva was striking: lean, muscular, and an enticing shade of blue. He wore a tiger-skin as a loincloth. Some of his dark hair was piled up in a topknot, and the rest fell to his shoulders. A thin jet of water — the holy river Ganga — flowed out of the topknot. His hair ornament was a crescent moon. A cobra with a raised hood twisted around his neck. His forehead was marked by three horizontal strokes. In the middle was his third eye, closed at this time. Necklaces made of large brown seeds decorated his bare chest and arms.

So over-the-top, thought Amy. A second-generation Goan Canadian, born Christian, Amy was not religious, yet there was a little shrine chockablock with Hindu gods and goddesses in her kitchen. Her husband, Madan, a first-generation immigrant from India, was more traditional. When Madan's mother, who lived in India, had visited them for the first time a few months ago, she had brought along another reference to divinity — a multicoloured, illustrated storybook about Goddess Annapurna. Tara had taken to her granny and to Annapurna. Very soon, the book had become her favourite bedtime read.

Amy's eyes continued to rest on Shiva. Tara tugged at her arm. Kissing Tara on her forehead, Amy opened the book.

"Roll, roll, roll away. Roll away to vic-to-ry," Parvati chanted as she rolled the dice, her eyes bright.

"Can we have some silence?" asked Shiva.

He lay on his side on a low divan, the fireplace behind him emitting an orange glow. He had lost a little money, nothing substantial. The dice fell on the low table between them. Parvati won again. Shiva frowned. "Bet on something more interesting this time," she said.

"Such as?"

"Why not your begging bowl?"

"No!"

"Oh, come on, Mighty One." She placed a gold and ruby earring on the table. "My wager's worth much more."

"In terms of money, yes; in terms of significance, no," Shiva responded grimly. He picked up his begging bowl with great deliberation and placed it on the table.

Parvati smiled. Shiva rolled the dice and lost.

"You must be cheating! How can you win all the time?"

Parvati smiled. She reached for her brass betel nut box. Taking out a betel leaf, she smeared it with slaked lime. In went slivers of betel nuts and some other goodies. Folding the leaf into a compact triangle, she held out the paan to Shiva, a peace offering he reluctantly accepted.

Lord Shiva and Lord Vishnu were on a leisurely stroll on the shore of Lake Manasarovar, in the high Himalayas. On the opposite shore of the pristine lake rose a range of ash-grey mountains, and towering above them was the impressive snow-clad Mount Kailash — Shiva's home.

"There's a splendid cave in one of the lower ranges where I meditated for eons. It was so beautiful and serene," said Shiva.

"Do you miss it?" asked Vishnu.

"I do, at times. The life of the spirit, you know. The one-pointed dedication to meditation. It was before marriage."

"Of course."

They walked on in companionable silence, enjoying the incandescent landscape of water, grassy stretches, and brown earth, domed by a cerulean sky that spread before them. There was no one else in sight. The air was cold, fresh, and pure.

Shiva was dressed, as usual, in his loincloth. He never felt cold and lived on the top of a mountain that was over six thousand metres above sea level. Vishnu, clad in flowing silk garments, was bejewelled. He had left his golden crown and the objects he usually held in his four hands — a spinning disc, a mace, a conch shell, a lotus — on Shiva's veranda. Married to Lakshmi, the goddess of prosperity, Vishnu missed his bachelor life. He was not a meditator; he was all action, having cycled gamely through ten avatars and a few others to spare. He had enjoyed a thrilling, ever-changing existence.

"Lakshmi seems ... well ... she seems so even-tempered," said Shiva.

Vishnu laughed magnanimously. "Appearances, you know what they say about appearances. But it's true, she can be calm."

"As for Parvati, she's been winning at dice all the time."

"I didn't know you played dice," said Vishnu untruthfully.

"We never used to. But then Narada dropped in one day and taught us to play."

Vishnu shook his head. Bad news always, that Narada.

"I have wagered my bowl and my trident and even my moon away," Shiva continued despondently. "I'll have to figure out how to get them back. Particularly my begging bowl. My annual pilgrimage is coming up soon."

"Don't worry, I'll help. You'll have them all back in no time," said Vishnu.

Shiva smiled. "I'd really appreciate that."

They walked on, contemplative. It would soon be sunset, and the last rays emitted by Surya, the sun god, would transform Mount Kailash into a shimmering mountain of gold.

Parvati awoke late to the sound of celestial birdsong. She lay in bed, uplifted by the melody. There were no birds on the summit of Mount Kailash. You had to descend to the foothills to meet them, as well as small scurrying animals, clumps of grass, wind-braving bushes, and an occasional stunted tree.

As the daughter of Himvat, god of the Himalayas, Parvati was at home in the snow. As a child she had rolled and cavorted in it, becoming intimate with its many moods and textures. As a goddess she had travelled a lot, visiting the tropics, forests, and oceans of sand, as well as countless temples, palatial homes, hovels, and humble huts of fisherfolk and farmers. Yet this was her first time in heaven, *swarg lok*. When she had arrived a few days earlier, the chief *dwarpal* at the door had taken her at once to see Indra, king of the highest heavens, God of gods. Wisps of cloud floated in and out Indra's palace, which rather resembled a labyrinth. Cotton-candy clouds were ever-present in heaven, giving it a romantic aura.

"Dearest Ma Parvati, what a great honour! How delightful to see you!" Indra gushed, springing up from his gold throne. "How's Shiva?"

"I hope you don't mind me visiting. I have always wanted to come," said Parvati.

"Of course, you're welcome. Consider this your home. I will ask Indrani to come and see you right away. She'll take care of all your needs."

Indrani, Indra's wife, the legendary queen, was reputed to be the most beautiful of all the goddesses.

"I'm sorry, but I'd prefer to be alone right now. I'd love to meet her later. I'm much in need of meditation, reflection, and time by myself," said Parvati.

"An excellent idea. One that we should all pursue. Unfortunately, there are always too many things to attend to," said Indra.

No doubt, given all the political intrigues you're involved in, thought Parvati, uncharitably. Folding her hands in a namaste, she took her leave.

The attendants brought her to a well-appointed room in a secluded part of the palace. Parvati sat down in a rocking chair, admiring the shocking pink bougainvillea blossoms that lined the spacious veranda. The attendants had thoughtfully left behind a glass of refreshing salt lassi. As she sipped the drink, her thoughts went back to the whole bloody mess that had brought her here.

Shiva and Parvati, Parvati and Shiva, were making love. At first, their lovemaking was high energy, even frenzied, but it gradually took on a slow, sensuous cadence. It cycled through various moods, emanating scents, music, and a kaleidoscope of colours. Their love play lasted for who knows how long, and it could have gone on for an eternity if Narada had not knocked on their door.

Shiva hastily put on his loincloth and went to greet Narada. They sat down, and Shiva offered his guest tea and snacks. Narada, as usual, was full of gossip from all three worlds — heaven, earth, and the underworld. It spilled out of him faster than words would allow. After a while he took some dice out of his pocket. "It's really quiet here. How about a dice game to liven things up?"

Narada explained the deceptively simple rules of a dice game. After they had played a few rounds, he took his leave. At the door he said, "If you lay a bet, it's really more fun." As Parvati turned away, he gave Shiva a wink.

Shiva and Parvati started playing dice every day. Life on earth was peaceful for the moment, and Shiva was not called upon to get rid of any malevolent forces. Parvati's work was also done for the season. Shiva and Parvati, Parvati and Shiva, were not given to idle pleasures, yet the dice game and betting drew them like a magnet. Greed, and the lust to win, claimed them both, but especially Parvati.

Parvati won and won some more. She had won everything and was feeling triumphant and invincible, but then she had lost and lost. She lost everything. Shiva happily reclaimed his begging bowl, his trident, and his crescent moon. Not that she would have kept them. She would have returned them if he had asked her nicely.

Later, Lord Vishnu paid them a visit and explained how he had moved the dice at his will. He had made her win and then he had made her lose. "It was all illusion, don't you see? It was *maya*," he said, with a charming smile.

"I should've known better than to give in to gambling," said Shiva.

Vishnu shrugged. He waved his hand in the air and held out a closed fist. "Can you guess what's inside?" he asked.

"Ashes," said Shiva.

"A pearl still nestling in its shell," said Parvati.

Vishnu opened his fist. A tiny pearl lay in its shell on a bed of ashes. He laughed. "Sometimes, it can be whatever you want it to be. But is it real or …"

Shiva and Parvati bowed low to the lord of preservation, who kept order in many worlds. After he left they decided to put the dice away. The day after, Parvati opened the windows to let in a blast of fresh snowy air and brewed some milky chai with tea leaves, cinnamon, cloves, fennel seeds, cardamom, a dash of ginger, and two spoons of sugar.

Shiva and Parvati sat at their low table, inhaling the fragrance of the steaming brew, looking through the large windows at clouds changing shape in the sky. Shiva reached across for Parvati's hand. Parvati smiled. Letting go, Shiva sat back and said, "You know, Parvati, there is a lesson in all this — Narada bringing us the dice game and Vishnu controlling our throws. All things material, like those dice, are *maya*. It's only consciousness that matters. This house, this divan that I sit on, even this warming tea you have made for us — it is all *maya*."

Parvati sat up. She had heard it all before. "The tea isn't *maya*. It's real. I am *prakriti*, nature; you are *purusha*, consciousness. We both matter, the material and the spiritual," she said.

"Only consciousness matters. Spirit. Soul. Mind. Everything else is of no importance. In fact it has no real existence."

Words piled high on words. Babel — a tower of words — arose between Shiva and Parvati, Parvati and Shiva. Shiva left soon after, saying that he had important matters to attend to. Parvati left as well. Demeaned, she had decided that she could not live in the same house as her husband. He had said that everything she stood for was of no importance, insisting that her domain, nature, was insubstantial. He had nullified her very existence and oh so casually.

At first Parvati found Indra's heaven thoroughly enchanting. One of her chief delights was encountering Airavata, Indra's celestial three-headed elephant, who passed by her veranda every morning, followed by an attendant. She wanted to go up to him, to bless him and be blessed by him. But all she could do was watch the imposing creature, who exuded such dignity, in awe. Looking at him, she thought, *Shiva's words that all material things are only* maya *are absurd. Would he dare to say that in the presence of Airavata?*

As time passed Parvati woke up with a feeling of discontent that she could not shake off. Her simple home was the very antithesis of this grandiose place called heaven. How she missed it! When she tried to meditate, she could not focus. Nor did she feel inclined to explore further, though she had discovered that there was no end to the diversions and entertainments in heaven. Parvati had longed to visit heaven, her curiosity aroused by the glowing descriptions of *swarg lok* from other gods and goddesses, but Shiva had turned down every invitation. *He would be a misfit here*, she thought. *Is that the reason he has not come to apologize and ask me to return home?*

From time-to-time Parvati looked down on earth from heaven. At first all was well. It was nice and relaxing to be in heaven. But one day she noticed that the plants on earth were drying up and dying. The next day she looked down again.

More trees and plants had died. Corn had stopped growing in the fields. The wheat and rice fields were also not doing well. *If this goes on, there will be a famine,* thought Parvati, *and everyone will starve.*

Days passed and the situation got worse. Since the farmers could not harvest their crops, the markets were empty. There was no food for the people to buy, nothing to cook. They were all hungry night and day. The children cried. They looked thin and pale and stopped playing.

I really need to do something, thought Ma Parvati. *Yes, I need to make a move.* Yet Parvati, ever purposeful, felt dazed and disoriented. *What has come over me?*

One morning Parvati decided to go for a walk in Nandanvan, the celebrated garden she had heard so much about. She needed to look upon something natural, something hopeful. The plants and trees, the birds and flowers, were not insubstantial — they were *prakriti*. They validated her existence.

She had barely slept the previous night. News from earth was horrifying, and her agitated thoughts had chased away any chance of repose. It was her absence that had turned abundance into scarcity. All things growing thrived through her benevolence, her caring touch. She was in charge of the entire harvest cycle after all. Yet she had walked away. She was guilty.

Why hasn't Shiva sent a message? He should have come days ago to plead with her to take her rightful place on earth to nurture the plants and trees, flowers, butterflies, and bees; to bless rain clouds and bring forth grain, vegetables, and fruits; to direct the winds so they brought bounty, not destruction.

She imagined Shiva wooing her, maybe in the presence of a witness or two. She had rehearsed what she would say. "But I don't exist, dear lord. I'm not pure consciousness. Since there is no material world, I am not needed, neither on earth nor in your home. The work I do is of no value at all." Angry, insolent words they would have been, but well deserved. So why hadn't he come?

"But what about you, Ma Parvati," said a small voice inside her. "What about your …? Are you …?" The voice had been getting more and more insistent. Idleness and the dereliction of duty were killing her.

Parvati walked toward Nandanvan and away from the torturous labyrinth of her thoughts. She entered a garden where butterflies and bees alighted on lovely flowers. Some still had dewdrops lingering on their petals. She was enchanted by the sacred trees that stood firm, combining strength, delicacy, and beauty. In the music garden, *apsaras*, heavenly entertainers, made sweet music and displayed their ethereal prowess at dance. *Everything in heaven has an airy vibe*, she mused. *Even Indra's throne, though it is made of solid gold.*

Turning a corner, she came upon a group of *apsaras* kneeling in a circle, worshipping Shiva. "We bow to you, Lord of the Universe, one who is Eternally Auspicious, Master of Destruction and Enabler of Recreation, Supreme Ascetic, One-Pointed Meditator …" they intoned.

Parvati fled.

The goddess descended to earth, stepping down in the holy city of Varanasi, which lay on the banks of the sacred river Ganga. There was no one on the streets. Parvati promptly sent out thought waves that summoned everyone to a public garden, and they came in hordes. Her heart went out to them. How thin they were! Hollowed out, haggard. She should have come sooner, much sooner. "Do not worry, my people. Your troubles are about to end. I will make khichari for everyone," her voice boomed and echoed.

Seeing Ma Parvati standing before them, people folded their hands, fell to their knees, bowed, and prostrated themselves. Turning to those closest to her, she asked them to get kindling and water, as well as pots, knives, spoons, and ladles. "Let's get a few fires going."

As people hurried away to do her bidding, a little boy standing by her side asked, "What will we cook with?"

The goddess smiled. "Mother Earth, I beseech you to give us rice," she said.

The people watched, barely breathing. Nothing happened for a few moments. Then a mountain of rice appeared behind the goddess, and a cheer rose through the crowd. Soon a mountain of toor dal appeared. Smaller heaps of onions, ginger, and garlic were followed by larger heaps of cauliflower, carrots, potatoes, and other ingredients. The people had not seen any food for weeks and weeks. If it hadn't been for the presence of the goddess, they would have made a run for the food. Silently, they watched, with hunger as well as hope.

"But where are the spices?" asked the little boy.

"An impatient little fella, aren't you?" said Parvati, smiling. "Cloud God, rain down golden turmeric," she commanded.

A shower fell, and everything was covered in a fine dust of yellow ochre. Some people started coughing and sneezing, others licked their fingers, and many clapped. Parvati asked for bright red chilies, peppercorns, cumin, fenugreek, cinnamon sticks, cloves, cardamom, and bay leaves. The spices appeared in orderly little heaps, and the child let out a sigh of relief.

Chanting a few magic words, Parvati sped up the cooking process so that everyone — old and young, children, women with babes on their hips, stray dogs, even a mangy cat or two — lined up. The people held up their plates to the pots of steaming khichari, oh so aromatic.

"Don't forget to put a good dollop of ghee on top. We need to get some flesh on those bones," Parvati reminded the servers.

She stood by a pot, serving everyone with her ladle and blessing them as well. Around her, volunteers continued to make more khichari. Nearby villages had heard about Parvati's soup kitchen, and more people joined the line. The day passed, and sunset loomed over the horizon. Parvati still stood at her pot, serving.

Suddenly, Shiva stood before her. She stared — speechless and overjoyed. He held out his begging bowl. "Ma Parvati, food is not an illusion. It is needed to nourish the body where the soul, the spirit, and the mind all live. Forgive me. I was wrong. Please come home. *Purusha* is incomplete without *prakriti*."

Parvati filled his bowl to the brim. Handing her ladle to an assistant, she sat Shiva down under a mango tree. Shiva and Parvati started feeding each other.

"Really, Parvati, your khichari is extraordinary! How I have missed your cooking. Your cooking surpasses …"

"Shhhh, enough flattery for one day," said Parvati.

They then fell to laughing.

"From that day, Parvati came to be called Annapurna, the giver of nourishment," Amy read. "In Varanasi, they built a temple to Annapurna. Other temples dedicated to her followed. And a Himalayan mountain range was named after her.

"For years to come, people talked about Parvati's khichari. Never had khichari been so delicious, so nourishing. The women tried to recreate that taste and flavour, that aroma, but they always fell a little short. 'Come on, how can you compete with a goddess? That, too, Ma Parvati?' their husbands teased. That's when some of them got chased out of the kitchen by their feisty, ladle-yielding wives."

Amy closed the book. *Well, it is actually a satisfying read*, she thought. After putting Tara to bed, Amy settled down in her study again, her thoughts turning to Tara's fascination with Annapurna. Maybe Tara had a bond with Annapurna because she, like Tara's grandmother, wore a saree? Tara had become very attached to her grandmother during her month-long stay. She had cried and been cranky for a few days after she left. *We could take her to India next year*, Amy thought. *I have that conference in Sri Lanka anyway.*

"Do you think it's all right for her to be so into Annapurna?" Amy had asked Madan. "I mean, it's one role model, Mother Goddess and all that. It's a good one, but there are others."

"You're overthinking it," Madan had responded. "I asked for the same story again and again when I was small. I don't even recall what it was. Something quite silly."

"And you turned out okay," Amy had responded teasingly.

Amy decided to reward herself with a glass of milk before going to bed. She had set it aside for Tara, then forgotten to give it to her. She would warm it in the microwave, add some chai masala powder, and just a hint of honey. A good recompense. But she had to earn it.

For the next two hours, she continued to mark papers. She was as focused as a moonbeam. She came to when she got a whiff of the spice mix used for chai — cinnamon, cloves, fennel seeds, and cardamom, with a dash of ginger. When she looked up, there was a glass of the steaming, flavoured milk on the far edge of her desk. Her heart skipped a beat. Amy went to the door and looked into the living room. There was no one there.

GODDESS PARVATI'S BENGALI KHICHARI

A savoury dish with rice, lentils, and vegetables

Vegetarian/Vegan, gluten-free
Servings: 6 | Cook Time: 50 minutes, approximately |
Level: Medium

INGREDIENTS

- 1 cup white basmati rice
- 1 cup masur/masoor dal (pink/red lentils)
- 2 tablespoons cooking oil
- ½ cup onion, chopped into ½-inch squares
- ½ teaspoon salt (to taste)
- ½ tablespoon ginger, grated or finely chopped
- ½ tablespoon garlic, grated or minced
- 2 cups mixed vegetables (see note), chopped into 1-inch pieces
- 4 cups water

Spices to fry:

  4 bay leaves
  3 cloves
  3 cardamom pods
  2 cinnamon sticks, 1 inch each
  1 teaspoon cumin seeds
  ½ teaspoon turmeric powder

Spices to add later:

  ½–1 teaspoon garam masala (to taste)
  ¼ teaspoon red chili powder (to taste)
  6 black pepper pods (optional)

For the garnish:

  1–2 tablespoons ghee or coconut oil, per serving
  Fresh cilantro, finely chopped

METHOD

1. This recipe comes together quickly, so make sure all your ingredients are ready before you begin. Measure and mix the rice and dal in a container and rinse twice. Drain and set aside. Measure 4 cups of water and set aside. Measure out all the spices to fry into a bowl and the rest of the spices into a second one. Keep the chopped onions close at hand.

2. Add oil to a large thick-bottomed pot and turn heat to high. As the oil starts to heat, add the spices to fry. As soon as the cumin starts sizzling,

turn down the heat and add the onions. Mix well. Turn heat to medium-high, add salt, and let the onions turn translucent. Add the chopped ginger and garlic. Mix well.

3. Add 2–3 tablespoons of water to prevent burning, if needed. When the mixture turns lightly brown and aromatic, add the vegetables and fry for 2 minutes. Add the rice-dal mixture and mix for 30 seconds. Add the remaining spices and the 4 cups of water. Mix, cover, and bring to boil. Turn heat to medium-low and let cook undisturbed for 20 minutes before checking. Cook until all water is absorbed. Remove from heat and leave covered for 5 minutes, then fluff with a fork.

4. Serve hot, garnished with fresh cilantro and a dollop of ghee or coconut oil, which should melt and blend into the khichari. Accompaniments include papadum, natural yogurt, pickles, and salad. Papadum can be oven-roasted or fried in oil.

NOTES

1. You can use potatoes, carrots, parsnips, turnips, cauliflower, broccoli, green pepper (or other peppers), peas, green beans, etc. It is a good idea to choose 2–3 vegetables. Some vegetables, chopped small, will cook sufficiently in this dish. But if you use dense vegetables, such as squash, lightly steam them before adding. Potatoes need to be parboiled beforehand, as they will not cook

sufficiently in the 20 minutes it takes for the rice-dal mixture to cook.
2. Indian cooking needs a cooking oil with a high-smoke point, such as sunflower, vegetable, or canola oil.
3. Always taste your garam masala to determine the heat level and adjust the quantity you add accordingly.

INTERLUDE

During my childhood in a small town in central India, I ate dishes from a regional vegetarian cuisine that came from the state of Maharashtra in western India. I never heard the word "curry" until my late teens. The word is a British invention to describe a dish with gravy. "Curry is, supposedly, Indian. But there is no such word in any of the country's many official languages,"[*] says the *Atlantic*.

According to Wikipedia,[**] curry comes from the Tamil word "kari," meaning sauce, i.e. gravy. These particular karis used curry leaves from the curry plant, not to be

---

[*] Nicola Twilley, Cynthia Graber, and *Gastropod*, "The Word *Curry* Came from a Colonial Misunderstanding," *Atlantic*, April 20, 2019, theatlantic.com/health/archive/2019/04/why-we-call-indian-dishes-curry-colonial-history/586828/#.

[**] Wikipedia, s.v. "Curry," last modified May 2, 2024, 18:08, en.wikipedia.org/wiki/Curry.

confused with the spice mixture curry powder. By the way, I recommend using curry leaves, which are available in many Indian stores. The word "curry" first appeared in a Portuguese cookbook in the mid-seventeenth century, put together by the British East India Company, which was trading with Tamil merchants. From these rather confusing beginnings, gravied dishes from India went on to conquer the world as curries. I sympathize with that catch-all invention — "curry" — as navigating between languages and cultures can be confusing, and the Indian subcontinent is particularly complex.

While researching for this book, I was led to "The World's Oldest Known Curry."[*] In 2010, archaeologists Arunima Kashyap and Steve Weber of Washington State University used a method called starch analysis to trace the world's first-known, or oldest, curry. They performed the analysis on the shards of a bowl found in a town called Farmana, not far from Delhi, the food capital of India. This town is part of a larger archeological site where the fascinating Harappan/Indus Valley civilization flourished some four thousand years ago, during the Bronze Age.

So, what did the Indus Valley dwellers eat? Lots of stuff, apparently: lentils and other pulses, wheat and barley,

---

[*] Soity Banerjee, "Cooking the World's Oldest Known Curry," *BBC News*, June 22, 2016, bbc.com/news/world-asia-india-36415079.

various fruits and vegetables, meat and fish.* No junk food, it seems.

I find it mind-boggling that modern science led us to this vegetable dish stuck to an ancient plate. But is it a curry? The jury is out on that one! We can, however, enjoy the reconstructed recipe.

---

* Jane McIntosh and Richard Meadow, "What Kinds of Things Did the Indus People Eat?," *Harrapa* (blog), n.d., harappa.com/answers/what-kinds-things-did-indus-people-eat.

"THE WORLD'S OLDEST CURRY"

A mellow, pleasing eggplant dish, adapted from Soity Banerjee's "The 'Original' Curry"

Vegan, gluten-free
Servings: 4 | Cook Time: 30 minutes | Level: Medium

INGREDIENTS

- 1 tablespoon ginger, roughly chopped
- ½ teaspoon turmeric powder
- ½ teaspoon cumin seeds
- 2-3 tablespoons sesame oil
- 4 cups eggplant, cubed
- ½ tsp salt (to taste)
- 1 tablespoon raw mango cubes or 1 teaspoon dry mango powder (amchur)
- 1 teaspoon cane or brown sugar

For the garnish:

- 4 tablespoons fresh basil leaves, finely chopped
- black pepper

METHOD

1. In a grinder or food processor, grind ginger, turmeric, and cumin seeds with a little bit of water to form a paste.
2. Heat sesame oil on medium heat, add the spice paste, and cook for 2 minutes. The spices will become aromatic. Add the eggplant and salt and stir well. Cover and cook on medium-high heat until the eggplant is nearly cooked through. Stir from time to time. Add a bit of water if needed to prevent sticking.
3. Stir in the raw mango (or mango powder) and the sugar. Cook covered on medium heat for 5 minutes or until eggplant is well cooked and soft. If using raw mango, it should have softened and cooked as well.
4. Remove from heat. Taste and adjust spices. Garnish with the chopped basil.
5. Sprinkle some black pepper on top and serve with naan, other Indian bread, or pita. This recipe also works well on quinoa or couscous. Add a chickpea salad to the meal for protein. Pepper is indigenous to India, and the Harappans likely knew it too!

NOTES

1. Asian eggplant works well for this dish. Make this dish when eggplant is in season in summer.
2. Dry mango powder, also called amchur, is available in Indian groceries.

DO THE RIGHT THING

Characters
Crow, a bird
Myna, a bird
Bhushan, a Hindu Brahmin
Mandakini, his Brahmin wife
Nathuram, an untouchable
Guru Nanak, the founder of Sikhism
Bhai Mardana, his Muslim companion

Myna and Crow sat side by side on a low branch of the shapely gulmohar tree. Spring was still a whisper away, and the buds that had sprouted plentifully had yet to burst into a riotous red. Early morning light diffused through the canopy into a compound with a little brick house, a well, a small vegetable garden, and a shed, where a cow grazed on some hay.

Mandakini, the seventeen-year-old lady of the house, was energetically sweeping the yard, humming a tune, the *pallu* of her saree sensibly tucked into her waistband. The exertion put a sheen of sweat on her oval face.

"Why don't we go eat, then come back?" Crow suggested. He wanted to fly into the undergrowth of a nearby thicket and breakfast on some tasty worms. For a change, there were no little ones to feed in his nest.

"Let's wait a bit," said Myna.

Crow squawked assent. He almost always agreed with Myna.

Bhushan appeared, wearing a spotless white *dhoti*, his upper body bare but for the sacred thread that went diagonally across his chest and left shoulder. His head was shaved, with only a tuft of hair left at the back, accentuating his high forehead and long face. As he chanted a Sanskrit prayer, Crow and Myna noted this special rhythm. Bhushan arranged the bricks that were neatly stacked against the wall into a clay cooking stove and laid out some firewood, preparing to cook the morning offering of khichari, rice mixed with masoor dal and scented with ghee. Every two weeks, his wife, Mandakini, made a fresh batch.

Crow's salivary glands came alive as he watched Bhushan. He loved the taste, the smell, the texture — everything, really — of the "yellow food." Some days the deliciousness ended up as food for the large four-legged, white animal that these humans kept. Despite her horns, this animal was nice and good at sharing. She allowed them to peck at the yellow food.

"Look how particular he is when he makes the yellow food," said Myna.

Crow squawked agreement. Bhushan washed the earthenware container, then wiped it meticulously with a white cloth, even as he continued to chant in a singsong voice.

"Oh, here comes that man who is always silent," said Crow in an excited voice.

Myna tightened her grip on the branch. She had a better sense of human speak than Crow and could mimic it a bit, though both grasped emotion and social interaction equally well. Sure enough, there was Nathuram, the *bhangi*, dressed in a slightly soiled *dhoti* and *kurta*, with a peaked white cap askew on his large head. Bhushan, having placed the pot on the fireplace, lit the fire with a touch of ceremony, since fire was sacred. He made his way out of the compound, head down, the prayers furious on his breath, almost colliding with Nathuram.

"Shiv, Shiv, Shiv! You muttonhead, can't you watch where you're going!" Bhushan yelled as Nathuram stepped away and stood looking down at the ground.

Mandakini rushed out of the house, her head covered with her *pallu*, to watch the end of a familiar scene. Here was a touch of drama in her humdrum life.

"Look, what you've done, you fool! Contaminated everything! Are you blind or what?"

Bhushan stalked off to bathe in the river for the second time that morning. He was expected at the moneylender's house, where he would look over the account books. The man did not trust his servant and always had the Brahmin double-check everything for a fee, and a rather handsome one. The moneylender would not berate Bhushan for being late, but Bhushan was fanatical about keeping his word.

After Bhushan left, Nathuram started cleaning the outhouse, which was set way back in the compound, while Mandakini buried the parboiled grains in the vegetable plot.

"Too bad the silent one came so early; otherwise, we'd have got the yellow food. Let's go eat, then?" said Crow. Having skipped breakfast, he was really hungry now.

"We can't yet. I'm going to report the loud one's mean behaviour to the man who understands us. It isn't right," said Myna grimly.

"What?" squawked Crow.

Myna flew off and Crow followed, cursing. Damn it all! Myna and her interfering ways. For all her sense of justice, she had thought nothing of laying her eggs in a nest he had built and letting him and his mate look after the hatchlings, with some help from their crow friends.

Guru Nanak was walking down a long, narrow road that ran between fields of lentils. He wore bright yellow robes and a turban to match. He was straight-backed and alert, and his luxuriant mustache and beard were dazzling white. A few steps ahead walked Bhai Mardana, dressed in shalwar pants and a *kurta*, carrying an Afghani lute called *rabab*. He strummed lightly on the strings, hardly aware of what he was doing. To Mardana, strumming on the *rabab* is the same as breathing, Guru Nanak often said.

A myna dived down from the sky and landed on Guru Nanak. Hearing the flutter of wings, Bhai Mardana turned and saw the bird sitting on Guru Nanak's left shoulder as a crow landed lightly on his other shoulder. Bhai Mardana smiled and kept walking. This was not surprising. Birds and animals sometimes visited Guru Nanak for a chat. After all, he was connected to everything in this world and beyond. His vision was vast, his consciousness all-encompassing. Guru Nanak did not break his stride either.

Myna made some sounds that were unintelligible to Bhai Mardana. *That bird is rather raucous*, he thought. After a couple of minutes, he heard Guru Nanak say, "Yes, yes, I understand. Don't worry."

A flutter of wings again, and Myna was gone, but Crow lingered. "Sometimes I wonder if the man who cleans the toilet irritates the one with the string on purpose," said Crow to Guru Nanak in a hesitant tone. "Is it possible?" he added.

"It could be the case," said Guru Nanak.

"Today we missed out on the yellow food," said Crow, sounding mournful.

"Come to the *langar*. There's plenty of food for everyone there," Guru Nanak suggested. Crow cocked his head.

"You haven't heard of the *langar*? I'm surprised," Guru Nanak said. He gave Crow directions on how to get there. Crow thanked Guru Nanak before flying off, for unlike Myna, he was well brought up.

"What did she say this time? And the crow? He doesn't usually speak," said Bhai Mardana.

Guru Nanak shrugged. "Nothing special. You know, birds will be birds."

Bhai Mardana let out a belly laugh. Guru Nanak looked pleased. He couldn't joke around with most people because everyone took him too seriously. He shared a true friendship with Bhai Mardana.

They entered a village, and a dozen men came up to pay their respects. They begged Guru Nanak to talk and teach. They offered the guests freshly made chapati — Indian flatbread — with a bit of oil spread on it and some salty buttermilk with a hint of asafoetida. Guru Nanak sat down on a *charpoy*, a string bed with a wooden frame, and gladly accepted the refreshments. The men lined up respectfully, and after he had eaten, they came up to him one by one.

"Should I, oh great guru, give up the worldly life and devote myself to Waheguru — God and wondrous teacher — leaving everything else behind?" asked the first.

"Spiritual life and everyday life are like two strands of a rope woven together. You are a married man with children, and a blacksmith, right? What is the need to renounce all that? Chant the name of Waheguru, make an honest living, share what you have with others, and love all living beings. Then salvation will be yours," said Guru Nanak.

The man bowed low and made way for another. After a while Bhai Mardana got up and wandered off. He started humming, strumming on the *rabab*, unmindful of his surroundings. New verses rose within him, wrapped in a melody like a spiral of smoke headed toward Waheguru. As Bhai Mardana entered a timeless realm familiar to wandering minstrels, his throat felt parched. Spotting a well just inside a compound, he found a small bucket of water perched on its rim; he tilted it toward his cupped hand and drank his fill.

Suddenly, he heard a roar as ferocious as a tiger's. "Thief, intruder, Mohammedan, how dare you barge in here! You have polluted my well, you imbecile! As if the stupidity of that idiot *bhangi* wasn't enough. Chicken-head, I will call the *havildar* and have you fined … I … I …"

Bhai Mardana turned around to face a Brahmin of medium height and build, red in the face.

"Maybe you need some water too? It could help you calm down."

Bhushan turned around, ready to explode again. Then he saw Guru Nanak and gasped. The serene old man who had materialized out of nowhere had an aura that conveyed high spiritual attainment. Bhushan had met a few gurus, godmen with spiritual powers, but none of them could hold a candle to this great soul.

Mandakini stepped out of the house, her head covered, thinking what an exciting day it was turning out to be. Seeing Guru Nanak, she stopped short, dazzled by the light that seemed to emanate from him. Recovering quickly, she stepped forward to touch the feet of this great sage who had graced their home.

"No, no, there is no need for that," he said.

"Are you ...?" she asked.

Guru Nanak folded his hands in a namaste. Mandakini was awed. She had heard so many stories about him. When Guru Nanak was a baby, his mother placed him under a tree, where a king cobra came to stand guard and shade his head from the fierce rays of the afternoon sun. The snake glided away as the petrified mother came to reclaim her son. Casting her a look, the cobra said, "As if I would ever strike such a Great One as He." In school at age seven, Guru Nanak told his teacher that the first letter of the alphabet resembled the number one, and this pointed to the unity of God. He later preached that God is the oneness that permeates all creation, and this oneness pervades the entire universe.

"Please have tea with us," she said earnestly to Guru Nanak, who nodded. She smiled at Bhai Mardana, who sat near the compound gate with the air of a man ready to let life take its own course.

DO THE RIGHT THING

Mandakini had heard stories about Guru Nanak's Muslim companion as well. Bhai Mardana and Guru Nanak came from the same village. Bhai Mardana's mother was terrified that she would lose him, for he was a sickly child, so she approached Guru Nanak for counsel. Though younger than Bhai Mardana by a few years, Guru Nanak took him under his wing. He improvised a string instrument with reeds and asked Bhai Mardana to play it. Bhai Mardana soon became an expert player and fell in love with making music. Music heals.

As Mandakini went about making tea, Guru Nanak turned decisively toward Bhushan. "I really don't understand your rude behaviour. Could you please explain it to me?" he asked.

Bhushan launched into a description of the purification rituals he performed every morning to cook food over a sacred fire, which he offered to the gods before he, and then Mandakini, ate. It was proper for Mandakini to eat only after her husband had had his meal. Of course, he had to do everything afresh every day. The ingredients he used were pure — no meat, fish, or eggs, and the rice was always cooked in ghee, which was made from the milk of the sacred cow.

"We must take care not to let someone from a low caste contaminate our food by his presence and particularly not an *achhut*, an untouchable, the lowest of the low. We must offer the purest food to God."

Guru Nanak heard him out and said, "I still don't understand. You clean everything so well to cook food that is so pure and sacred only to put it in a mouth polluted by curses and defiled by belittling other humans and a body dominated by a mind filled with anger and egotism. Surely, this sacred food deserves a mouth that is equally pure, a mouth that enunciates words that are kind and loving?"

Bhushan stared at Guru Nanak, then lowered his gaze. Mandakini looked up from the pot of water, milk, sugar, black tea, and cardamom pods that was merrily bubbling away. Her gaze went from Bhushan to Guru Nanak and back again.

Bhushan said nothing for a few minutes. "What you say makes sense, great guru. I have heard much about you, and I have also heard about your teachings, but I must say that I don't know enough to really understand them. I would be very obliged if you took a seat, accepted our hospitality, and explained them to me," he said gravely.

Guru Nanak looked at the earnest Brahmin who stood before him. He surmised that he was in his late twenties. It is always good to learn, and this is certainly a fitting age, he thought as he nodded.

Myna and Crow had been observing the scene from their perch. Myna gave Crow a triumphant look, which Crow acknowledged. Then they both made their way to the *langar* for lunch. The place was not far as the crow flies.

The next day Crow and Myna were back. Crow had eaten a hearty breakfast; the grasshoppers had been particularly delicious that morning. He wasn't exactly vegetarian, though he had developed a taste for spices.

From their perch they saw Mandakini stacking bricks and arranging the kindling to make a fire. She set a covered earthenware pot matter-of-factly on the fire. Crow and Myna exchanged glances. This woman never prepared the yellow food.

"I'll go look for the loud one with the string by the river," said Crow.

"Good idea," Myna responded.

Soon Crow was back to report that the man with the string was sitting on the bank in a strange posture — lower limbs crossed, back straight, hands resting on the upper part of the lower limbs, eyes shut. He and Myna had flown close to such humans, chirping and flapping their wings. Some opened their eyes and gave them angry looks, others were neutral, and a few seemed oblivious to their presence. Myna had let Crow know that she disapproved of creatures who were not conscious of their surroundings at all times.

"I don't think we'll get any yellow food. Let's check back tomorrow," said Crow. Myna agreed.

It was late afternoon when Bhushan returned home. He ate a banana for lunch. Every month he fasted on certain holy days. Some fasts were strict — no food or water — others allowed fruit. Then Bhushan opened a large battered-looking book of scripture written in Sanskrit and started reading. Mandakini glanced at him. She wondered what he was thinking. Was he, perhaps, disturbed by what Guru Nanak had said to him?

Scenes from Guru Nanak's visit kept flashing through her mind. She recalled how he had spoken with Bhushan for hours. She lost the thread of the conversation after a while, though she had picked up bits here and there. When Mandakini had started cooking lunch, Bhai Mardana began playing the *rabab* ever so softly. It was wonderful to have some music while she made chapatis and sabji, a dry vegetable dish with potatoes and eggplant. She served these with homemade yogurt and mango pickle.

Guru Nanak and Bhushan had eaten hastily. Bhai Mardana smacked his lips and asked for a second helping, declaring it was the best food he had ever had. Mandakini decided then and there that some of the things she had been told about Mohammedans needed to be taken with a pinch of salt. "No, no, this meal is nothing special," she protested. "If I had known that you and Guru Nanakji were coming, I would've planned something really nice."

"You are a *sugrihini*. No matter what you serve, it will always taste good. My wife is also like you," Bhai Mardana said.

Mandakini was overwhelmed. Her husband praised her cooking from time to time, but he had never called her a *sugrihini*. In fact nobody had. She cut open a papaya and handed two slices to Bhai Mardana, taking a couple for herself. As they enjoyed the perfectly ripened fruit, they smiled complicitly at each other, even as Guru Nanak and Bhushan continued to chew on words and concepts.

On the third day after Guru Nanak's visit, Bhushan emerged from his silence. "Do you know what Guru Nanakji told me? When he was nine, his father wanted him to have the sacred thread ceremony, as he felt he was mixing too easily with Mohammedans and low-caste kids. Many preparations were made for the event, and a lot of people were invited. When the priest arrived, he explained that the sacred thread symbolizes the transference of spiritual knowledge. Performing the sacred thread initiation opened the way for a Brahmin boy to understand the Vedas and other sacred texts and to perform purification rites and sacrifices, all of which would elevate him to the highest spiritual plane."

"And Guru Nanakji comes from the Vaishya caste, doesn't he?" Mandakini asked.

Bhushan nodded. Mandakini took up the story. "Guru Nanakji asked the Brahmin, 'While men from the three upper castes are allowed the sacred thread, why are all women, and boys from lower castes, not allowed to have the sacred thread ceremony? How is this fair?'"

Bhushan said, "'You must respect the scriptures,' said the priest, 'and not question them.' 'But how can I really understand the scriptures unless I ask questions?' Guru Nanakji said. 'Knowledge is the ultimate authority, not a human being, however learned. Anyone who wishes to walk on the spiritual path, who is eager to learn, should be allowed to do so.'"

Mandakini said, "They debated for a long time, but Guru Nanakji did not accept the sacred thread. The priest took his fees and left in a huff. The people who had gathered took Guru Nanakji's side and praised his wisdom, and everyone enjoyed the feast that had been prepared for the occasion."

Bhushan shook his head, chuckling. "He turned everything on its head."

"At the *dharmsala* in Katarpur, where Guru Nanakji gave his first teachings, there is a *langar*, the community kitchen. The faithful cook meals every day and serve them to everyone who comes, no matter their beliefs. I have heard that noblemen and paupers eat sitting side by side," said Mandakini.

Bhushan shook his head again. Giving alms and serving the poor was prescribed in their religion as well. A man of God who came to their door in his wanderings was never sent away without food or a coin. On certain holy days, and they were numerous, rich men sponsored temples to serve food to hundreds, sometimes thousands. But people of lower and higher castes eating together was simply unacceptable.

In the days that followed, Bhushan let Nathuram come and go as he pleased, even as he continued to cook khichari ceremonially every morning and offer it to the gods while chanting. Nathuram's behaviour changed as well. He started maintaining a distance from Bhushan as he went about his work. Since her husband seemed a bit less dogmatic and more

DO THE RIGHT THING

relaxed, Mandakini introduced a bold topic. "You know that Sharada goes to the *langar* every week," she said.

Sharada, the moneylender's daughter-in-law, was Mandakini's friend. Having miscarried her first child, she had fallen into a well of grief. Guru Nanak was consulted, and he recommended *seva*, selfless service, at the *langar*. Now she went every Saturday to cook there. In the community kitchen, she kept her head covered and her face averted from the men as she made hundreds of chapatis along with the other women volunteers.

"Yes, I know that. Why? Do you want to visit the *langar*?" Bhushan asked.

Mandakini blushed. "Well, no, not really. I mean, I am a little curious, especially now that Guru Nanakji has graced our home. But it wouldn't be right."

"You really want to go, don't you?"

Mandakini chastely cast her eyes down. She had travelled but once in her life. A year earlier, she had tied the sacred knot in her village, and Bhushan had brought her here — a two-day journey by bullock cart — as his bride. Bhushan had moved here five years before from his native village in the neighbouring province. The resident Brahmin had passed away, and a replacement was needed to perform priestly duties at weddings, births, funerals, and other rituals and festivals. The job offer had come to him though a distant uncle.

Playing with the end of her *pallu*, Mandakini stood daydreaming. She and Sharada would take a ferry across the river, then get into the donkey cart that the moneylender arranged. She had never been on a ferry or in a donkey cart. What an adventure it would be! Sharada had also told her that on the way, there was a Yakshi temple. There had been one in Mandakini's village, and she had prayed there regularly with her sisters, receiving the Yakshi's blessings. She longed for a *darshan* of this ancient and ferocious-looking female divine who presided over plants and pregnancies — all things that take root and grow. Mandakini missed the Yakshi.

Bhushan was also lost in thought. He recalled Guru Nanak's words, "Those who do *seva*, without thought of reward, will attain liberation. *Seva* brings as much peace as prayer and meditation." *Seva had worked for Sharada*, he mused, *for she had started to emerge, slowly, from her melancholia.* "Go with her then. Just make sure that all the housework is taken care of," he said to his wife.

Mandakini nodded, her eyes shining. She wanted to skip around and sing out loud, but that would have to wait. She was no longer at her parents' home, her hair in girlish braids, joking and laughing with her sisters. She decided that she would make Bhushan his favourite dal that evening. It would turn out well; she was a *sugrihini* after all.

"May I ask you something else?" she said.

"Of course, you know that you can always do that," Bhushan responded, smiling fondly at his wife.

"Somehow, I thought that you would be upset by what Guru Nanakji said. At least a little."

"He's a realized soul and brilliant. Guru Nanakji's teachings are new, and they are like a river — deep and nourishing — yet contained within the banks. In our religion, which goes far back to antiquity, there is a multiplicity of ideas and beliefs, ways of worshipping and living. It is an abundant ocean that receives everything and keeps expanding," Bhushan responded, his face glowing.

Mandakini narrowed her eyes as she tried to take it all in. She had a feeling that Bhushan was right. She loved many gods and goddesses; Goddess Annapurna, Lord Shiva, and Krishna were her favourites. She also enjoyed the many festivals and rituals, particularly Holi. It started with the burning of the demoness Simhika in a huge bonfire that lit up the night sky, followed the next day by the exuberant play with colours that drenched the world in myriad hues. The songs and the stories of gods and goddesses reverberated through her. As for the Yakshi, she was certain that she watched over her.

"I'll go and see Sharada. I'll be back soon," she said.

Myna and Crow were listening to this exchange between Bhushan and Mandakini.

"Do you think she will cook at the *langar*?" Crow asked.

"Maybe."

"Perhaps she'll make the yellow food."

"Perhaps."

Crow looked pleased as he took to the sky with Myna. Chick season was upon them again, and the coming weeks would be very busy. It was hard work to keep their little nestlings well fed, but Crow and Myna would not have it any other way.

MANDAKINI'S DAL

A nourishing spiced lentil dish from North India

Vegan, gluten-free
Servings: 4 | Cook Time: 30 minutes | Level: Easy

INGREDIENTS

- 1 cup masur (pink lentils)
- 3½–4 cups water
- 1–2 tablespoons cooking oil
- ½ heaped teaspoon cumin seeds
- 1 large onion, chopped into ½-inch pieces
- ½ teaspoon turmeric powder
- ½ teaspoon salt (to taste)
- 1 tablespoon ginger, grated or finely chopped (or ready-made paste)
- 1 tablespoon garlic, finely chopped (or ready-made paste)
- 1 medium tomato, chopped into ½-inch pieces (or equivalent canned tomatoes)
- 1 teaspoon coriander powder
- 1 teaspoon dry mango powder (amchur) or 1 tablespoon lemon juice
- ½ teaspoon garam masala (to taste)
- ¼ teaspoon red chili powder (to taste)

METHOD

1. Wash lentils, but do not soak them.
2. Put lentils in a large pot and add 3½–4 cups of water. Bring to a high boil, half covered. (Monitor the dal, as it can easily run over, since pink lentils expand a lot when boiled.) The boiling will create foam on top, which should be taken off with a ladle. This step can also be done in either a slow cooker or a pressure cooker.
3. Once the dal starts boiling, turn heat to medium-high. Turn off the heat when the dal is very soft. With a whisk or fork, carefully whip the hot dal into a soup-like consistency. Thickness of dal is a personal preference.
4. Heat oil in a thick-bottomed pot on high heat and add cumin seeds. As the cumin starts sizzling, turn down the heat and add the onion, turmeric, and salt. Turn up the heat to medium-high and fry until the onion starts to darken. If the mixture starts sticking to the pot, add some water.
5. Add ginger and garlic and fry well. Add cooked lentils, tomatoes, coriander powder, dry mango powder or lemon juice, garam masala, and red chili powder. Bring to a boil on medium-high heat, uncovered. Simmer for at least 5 minutes, stirring every now and then. Taste and adjust the salt, garam masala, and chili powder.
6. Serve as a savoury soup or as a main dish with rice. Accompaniments include a salad, papadum, natural yogurt, pickles, and chutneys.

NOTES

1. Indian cooking needs a cooking oil with a high-smoke point, such as sunflower, vegetable, or canola oil.
2. Always taste your garam masala to determine the heat level and adjust the quantity you add accordingly. The heat/chili level varies.
3. To convert this recipe to a one-dish meal, add 2 cups of mixed vegetables. Chop and steam or microwave the vegetables very lightly while boiling the dal and add them along with the other ingredients in step 5.
4. Keeps well in the fridge for 2-3 days. The flavour improves overnight!

THE FISHERMAN AND THE SORCERESS

Characters
Ijay, a fisherman
Bhuvana, a sorceress
Kadeem, a boy in Ijay's village

Ijay squatted by his father's boat, smoking a *beedi*. This simple, local cigarette was the last one he had rolled before running out of tobacco. He had no money to buy more. Nor could he cadge from anyone, because he owed everyone, and he did not just owe *beedis*.

He wished he had some tobacco. The leaves to roll it in could be found in the woods, and he knew how to create a spark by striking stone to stone. All he needed was a little tobacco, just a little bit. He wished for many things, but none of his wishes came true.

He saw a circle of men a little way off on the beach, drinking toddy, the local hooch, talking loudly, and laughing — his father and brother among them. But he could not join their circle. It was getting dark. Soon the tips of their *beedis* would glow red in the gloom.

A familiar hunger-anger gnawed at him. Every day he took a boat out to sea at dawn and sat in it, with a line thrown overboard. There was usually an old, weather-beaten boat available that no one wanted. The rest of the fishermen caught fish, even big fish, while he caught nothing. Ijay cast his nets just like the other fishermen. While their nets would be heavy with fish, he would find only a handful in his. Cursed he was, accursed to the core. The rare day when he felt a tug on the line and slowly started reeling it in, he would feel the fish suddenly jerk away. When the line came up empty, the hook, dangling free, mocked Ijay. Every time the fish escaped, he experienced shame, a shame that had lodged deep within.

All the fishermen were busy — looking after their nets and boats, fishing, going to the market — their lives entangled with those of their wives and children, brothers and sisters, parents and grandparents, aunts and uncles, and friends. He watched this gregarious parade of daily life from the sidelines. The fishermen did not want him around, afraid that they might catch his bad luck. Ijay kept away from them as much as he could. He avoided his family, creeping into their hut when his father and brother were asleep and leaving before they awoke.

As Ijay ran his hand along the rough wood of his father's boat, he was invaded by despair. He did not have his own boat when even the humblest fisherman in the village had a small rough-and-tumble craft to call his own. He was of marriageable age but had no wife. Who would give his daughter to such a loser?

Ijay was just coming to, aware that he was in an enclosed space. Opening his eyes momentarily, his gaze encountered a round roof. He tried to focus, but his eyes closed and he drifted off. After a while he came to again. This time he took in the carefully woven criss-cross pattern of the roof. He found himself thinking that it must be very early.

He had come to Bhuvana at midnight. She lived apart from the rest of the village, in the woods, a thorny fence marking her territory. She was a witch, herbalist, and midwife all rolled into one. Desperation had driven Ijay into her lair. Desperation, hunger, and shame that pushed his head down. The unspoken accusations of his father and brother echoed in his mind. He was not entitled to food, not to toddy, not to tobacco. Not even to his sleeping mat. When he came to see Bhuvana, she welcomed him. She understood his problem at once, though the words were scarcely out of his mouth, and offered a solution. Bhuvana had wrought her magic, magic black as the ever-churning sea on a moonless night. But would it work?

They had sat on opposite sides of the fire, Bhuvana chanting, low and guttural. Ijay leaned toward the fire, drinking a brew she had given him. Her voice rose steadily, the sound harsh in his ears, even as he started to feel woozy, his vision blurring. He thought he heard the cries of a wild animal. Jackal? Hyena? Perhaps the sounds were emanating from Bhuvana herself? Were there animals prancing around the fire? Was he the wild-haired man madly dancing? Could he have somehow plunged into the inky black sea? No, it was all magic, Bhuvana's black magic.

Ijay became very afraid. He wanted to run away, but the drink had paralyzed him. With a cunning little knife, Bhuvana had made a cut in his middle finger and commanded him to let the blood drip into a small fire in the middle of her compound. He had sworn that he would give her a part of his harvest from the sea for the next six months. They sealed their pact in blood. Of what transpired after, he recalled but fragments. He remembered her voice had reached such a crescendo that, before passing out, he thought his head would explode.

Every day there was bounty. Ijay brought in tons of fish, small and big, and not just fish but also shrimp, octopus, calamari, lobster. Sometimes there was even a sea turtle — an expensive delicacy — or a manta ray. How he made these great catches was a mystery. He went a long way down the coast to fish. Usually, he was gone all night. Rumours circulated, but people only whispered.

Ijay now looked people straight in the eye, but they turned away. He bought a boat and some clothes. He got his long locks and beard trimmed, becoming civilized. He gave packets of tobacco to all the men in the village. He gave the children toffees and sweets. The attitude of the young women changed. Their eyes became as eloquent as their hips. Success stoked desire, and Ijay started going to a brothel in town. He was not going to choose a village woman as his wife. In the past they had acted as if he did not exist. Perhaps he would find a mate in another village. But it wasn't yet time. He had to pay off his debt to Bhuvana.

Though success put a shine on Ijay's face and flesh on his body, there was one thing he hated. He dreaded going to Bhuvana's compound to make payments. She was greedy and asked him to get her something special, a sea urchin or an eel. Ijay pressed back. The deal was fish, he said. Then Bhuvana looked malevolently at him, saying nothing.

"I'll see," Ijay would mutter, turning quickly away, suddenly afraid.

The villagers decided not to pry into Ijay's affairs, but Kadeem thought otherwise. He decided to follow him one dark, moonless night.

Ijay looked back from time to time as he walked, but he did not see the quick dark-skinned boy who kept to the plants that lined the shore.

After some time Ijay stopped by a crumbling brick wall. The abandoned structure had fallen into decay a long time ago. Here he dropped the fishing net that he had slung over his shoulder. Kadeem could not see him for a moment as Ijay crouched down. Then Ijay stood up and ran straight into the sea. He was naked, and headless. Yes! Ijay had no head.

Kadeem cowered behind a bush, silently reciting prayers that his grandfather had taught him. He was terrified. He tried not to look at the head that sat by itself on the sand, with Ijay's loincloth lying next to it.

After a while Ijay returned. He stood on his hands, near the head, so that his legs were up in the air and his neck pointed down. Before the boy's astonished eyes, a stream of fish escaped from Ijay's neck cavity and poured onto the sand. Then Ijay got back on his feet, replaced his head, dressed, gathered the fish into his net, and started dragging his haul back home.

After that night, Kadeem made it a point to avoid Ijay. Surely, the man was in communion with evil spirits. Yet curiosity and greed proved stronger than fear. A month later, when the new moon cast the world into obscurity, Kadeem followed Ijay again. The head had magical powers. Could he use it to get some sweets? Or one of those wind-up toys? Why not a few coins?

Once again, Ijay dived into the sea, and Kadeem moved forward, slow and stealthy. When he saw the head sitting on the beach, he felt nauseous, but he forced himself to pick it up. It was heavy. He held it by the hair at an arm's length and started back home, refusing to look at it. As he walked, going as fast as he could, the head seemed to get heavier. He was not very far from the village when he cast a look at the head. Ijay's eyes bored into him; they were alive, glowing! Terrified, he started running, but soon he stumbled and the head fell and rolled away. When he picked himself up, he kicked the head toward a line of beach grass and ran home, kicking up sand, panting.

When Ijay discovered that his head had disappeared, he began a frantic search. He was able to sense everything acutely, even without his head. The search was futile. *A rogue wave must have carried it away*, he thought. *Will I ever be able to find it again?*

Sweating and weary, he sat down on a large rock. Dawn was not far off. The sun would rise soon and yet another day would begin. Terrifying thoughts penetrated his consciousness. *Do I really need my head? What am I thinking? Of course I need my head! Am I still a human being?* He cried out loud and beat his fists on the rock.

During the day, while walking on earth, he longed to be united with the sea. He imagined the gradations of luminosity, the light descending from a surface painted in shades of blue and green to a zone simplified into grey and black before the darkness deepened. Under the surface there were plains and plateaus, mountains and valleys, just like on land. He wanted to explore that strange, new world and understand its secrets. He wanted to make it his own. The more time he spent underwater, the less at ease he felt on land and among the villagers.

There were no words under the waves and hardly any sounds, though he could hear himself breathing and all his senses were sharper, while on land, words and thoughts clouded everything. Sensations travelled easily in that watery world. It aroused feelings and evoked ideas, all new, elusive yet alluring. For a visitor, it opened up a magical world of fish and plants and legless wonders, smooth their bodies, hairless, graceful their movements. Enticingly strange and secret was this world, but oh, so very lovely.

The ocean was infinite, teeming with creatures large and small, all of whom seemed more noble than earthly beings. Ijay was seized by a thought — *Could the ocean become my home? A headless man cannot live among people, but perhaps I would be accepted in the ocean?* He had grown up on tales of *matsya kanyas*, mermaids, told by fishermen who had seen them with their own eyes. It was always a lone figure perched on a lone rock along the deserted coastline of a tiny island. Attractive they were, these *matsya kanyas*, with their long, wet hair floating around them. As they steered their boats closer, the fishermen noticed that their shapely bodies ended in a fishy tail. After the fishermen caught but a glimpse, the creatures would disappear into the sea.

The teacher in the nearby town had scoffed at these accounts, calling them wild tales of unschooled and unreliable minds that were likely affected by too much toddy, or worse, but most of the villagers held fast to them. They believed that *matsya kanyas* and their male counterparts, *matsya kumars*, lived somewhere in the depths. These stories had entered Ijay's head through one ear and gone out the other. He had found them inconsequential, occupied as he was with his inability to catch any fish. Now he wondered if there was some truth in them.

The bounty I had was all because of magic, Bhuvana's terrible black magic, Ijay thought. He shuddered; he had never reconciled to that. *On land, I will always be in her power, but the ocean has its own laws. There, I would be beyond her reach.*

Ijay hid in the bushes. He was exhausted and dozed off until dawn. He awakened with a start and longed to feel the light, warmth, and energy of the sun. The one thing he would miss down in the depths was that almighty ball of fire, just as he would miss the silver moon, shining with its cold, delightful intensity in a midnight sky. *Yet I could still rise to the surface sometimes*, he thought. The sun rose slowly and magnificently over the world, filling it with radiance. Ijay sought the blessings of Surya, the sun god, and having received them, plunged into the sea.

Next morning, Kadeem awoke, guilt stricken. Hesitatingly, he confessed all to his gentle grandfather, who took him at once to see Ijay's father. Kadeem led the two men to the spot on the beach where he had left the head. But there was no head. Instead, they found a tree, tall and graceful, with swaying fronds at the top, the wind singing softly as it flowed through the fan-like leaves.

A couple of months after this discovery, the villagers noticed a cluster of green fruits at the top of the tree, just under the lovely fronds. One of them fell to earth. When the people broke it open, there was water inside, sweet and refreshing, and the shell was lined with thick white flesh, also delicious. They started harvesting the fruit, which they named "nariyal," coconut. Along the coastline that bordered Ijay's village, the lone tree that had sprung up on the shore engendered other trees, lining the beach with coconut palms, their fronds making music with the breeze. Soon it seemed as if they had always been there.

THE FISHERMAN AND THE SORCERESS 129

One day a woman left a green coconut under an upturned basket at the back of her hut and forgot about it. When she found it again, it looked discoloured and a little shrivelled. Something compelled her to take all the fibre off with a sickle. Inside was a slightly hairy brown nut that looked like a face. She took the coconut around the village. "Look, it's Ijay's head," she told everyone, and the people nodded in agreement.

Late at night, under the cover of dark, the villagers would speculate about Ijay's fate. Some people didn't care very much and yawned when the subject came up. Others shrugged and accepted that they would never know. A handful were obsessed with the unfinished story. They would go into a little huddle on the beach, spinning tales and theories, each new one more fanciful than the last. The villagers passed Ijay's story from one generation to the next, even as they feasted on spicy coconut curries, gingery coconut chutneys, and coconut sweets scented with cardamom. The empty coconut shells became containers, and the brown fibre was converted into rope, mats, brushes, brooms, and scrubbers. The villagers remembered Ijay for the bounty he had provided and thanked him for his generosity.

Kadeem thought about Ijay every day. As he grew to be a man, the weight of guilt continued to haunt him. At the mosque he prayed for forgiveness and for Ijay's well-being. He joined his father's profession and became a potter. He donated generously to the mosque and to his community, which brought him some relief. Then Kadeem got married, and when his first-born — a son — came into this world, he named him Ijay.

AVIAL

Vegetables in a zesty coconut sauce

Vegetarian, gluten-free, contains nuts
Servings: 4–6 | Cook Time: 35 minutes | Level: Easy

INGREDIENTS

4 cups mixed vegetables, chopped into
   1-inch pieces
¼ cup raw cashews (optional)
1½ cups natural yogurt (3½% or 2%)
1½ cups canned coconut cream
1 small hot green chili, finely chopped (to taste)
1½ teaspoons Madras curry powder (to taste)
½ teaspoon salt (to taste)
¼ teaspoon crushed black pepper (to taste)

Spices to fry:

2 tablespoons coconut oil
1 teaspoon cumin seeds
½ teaspoon turmeric powder
6–8 fresh curry leaves

METHOD

1. Lightly steam the vegetables, along with the cashews, if using. Set aside.
2. Gently fold yogurt and coconut cream together in a large bowl. Add the hot green chili, curry powder, salt, and black pepper. Add vegetables and mix well. Set aside.
3. In a small thick-bottomed pot, heat the coconut oil and add the cumin seeds and turmeric powder. When they start sizzling, add curry leaves. Stir and remove from heat. Add the fried spices to the mix of vegetables, coconut cream, and yogurt. Mix well.
4. Serve on white basmati or brown rice. Good accompaniments are Indian pickles, chutneys, and papadums.
5. This dish can be refrigerated and used over 2–3 days. Serve chilled on a hot day or at room temperature year-round.

NOTES

1. Use coconut milk if you cannot find coconut cream.
2. A variety of vegetables can be used in this dish: root vegetables, such as carrots, potatoes, parsnips, squash, turnips, and radishes; green or yellow beans; cabbage; peas; cauliflower; green pepper; and zucchini. Try to combine sweet, subtle, and strong flavours when choosing the vegetables. I suggest using no more than 4 different ones.

THE FISHERMAN AND THE SORCERESS

3. Use a yogurt brand that is a bit sour, or add a couple of drops of lemon juice to the yogurt if it is not sour. More coconut cream will give a sweeter flavour. More yogurt will give a tangier taste.
4. Since the chili may cause a burning sensation on exposed skin, wear rubber gloves when chopping. In Indian cooking we do not deseed green chilies.
5. Sometimes I skip the green chili and add more crushed black pepper. It's worth buying Indian black pepper from an Indian store, as it's more flavourful.
6. Buy fresh curry leaves in an Indian shop. Remove stems and freeze the leaves in an airtight container. Defrost before using.

CHEF WILLIAM AND CAPTAIN TYRANT

Characters
William Harold, an English chef
Captain Henry Spears, William's employer
Miranda Spears, the captain's wife
Mrs. Manly, Miranda's lady's maid
Mrs. Khambatta, a Parsi lady
Celeste Knight, William's former employer
Rory, William's friend
Edwina, William's ex-fiancée

As William Harold walked down the dusty road, he dripped with sweat. His thin white cotton shirt stuck to his back. Sweat plastered his auburn hair against his forehead, and the heat created reddish blotches on his cheeks. The extreme weather parched his throat, slowed his steps, and sucked up his energy. It was well past noon. He had forgotten his hat at home, and he never carried a flask of water. A thought formed in his sluggish brain: *Dante's Inferno isn't hell; hell is right here in this cantonment town on this blistering North Indian plain.*

The day had begun normally enough. He had risen early and spent some time planning the week ahead with the head cook in the mess kitchen. Then he served Captain Henry Spears a late breakfast of chicken cutlet, fried eggs, toast, and tea. He always ate the same thing every morning.

"I had something rather good lately, William, and I'd like to have it for dinner," said Spears as William started clearing up the dishes.

"What was it, sir?"

"Has a peculiar name: bhel. B-H-E-L. Very spicy and altogether different."

"Where did you eat it?

"When I was visiting Almigarh last week. We were invited to the house of this trader who I believe was Gujarati. It's a popular dish, I'm told. You'll find the recipe by asking around."

"That I will do, gladly. I'll see if I can get the recipe. It may take a little while to find all the ingredients."

"Oh, come on, William! What a fuss about nothing! I want you to serve bhel tonight and then for the troops tomorrow at lunch as an appetizer. The men haven't been in a good mood lately. They need some spicing up."

When William left home that morning, Mrs. Manly told him not to worry about a thing. Of course she would check the deliveries and ensure everything else was in order. Mrs. Manly was Mrs. Spears's lady's maid. Since Mrs. Spears had migraines and spent most days lying in her darkened bedroom, Mrs. Manly had little to do.

William started out right away to find the recipe. His first stop was the nawab's luxurious *haveli*. He spoke to the head cook, whom he knew. The man responded that he had only a vague knowledge of the dish. The two men conversed in Hindi.

"I know they use muri. You know muri?" asked the cook.

"Yes," said William. Muri was puffed rice.

"And there're many other things in it. It's a dish from Bombay. Why don't you go to Mr. Khambatta's house?"

The Parsi community had links with Bombay, and Mr. Khambatta was a prominent Parsi businessman. William went over at once, and the servant fetched the lady of the house. Mrs. Khambatta, tall and dignified, was draped in an elegant saree. "I do know what you're talking about, William. Yes, there is muri for sure. And potatoes and onions. There are some chutneys, and these are what really make the dish," Mrs. Khambatta said in fluent English.

"What kind of chutneys?"

"This, unfortunately, I don't know. You see, my mother was very traditional and strict, and she would never let us eat street food. I've eaten bhel, but neither my cook nor I have ever made it. I'm playing rummy with the ladies tomorrow, and I can ask them. I'm sure someone will know of the recipe."

"That is very kind, but Captain Spears insists on bhel for dinner tonight."

"Oh no! I'll ask the neighbours and send the boy over if I find out anything useful."

William thanked Mrs. Khambatta and turned to go. *What a good sort*, thought William as he walked down the long driveway to the gate. She reminded him of Celeste Knight, his mistress at Rose Hall when he first arrived in Mansubh. A year and a half earlier, William had left London a wounded man. Not wounded by war or the stock exchange but turned down by the woman he loved. Edwina, having accepted and then rejected his marriage proposal, evaded his questions and pleas and never gave a reason for breaking up.

After Mrs. Khambatta's house, William tried four more, including a Maharashtrian family. Since the Maharashtrians were originally from Bombay, this family would surely know about bhel. Unfortunately, the woman of the house was out of town. Still, he learned that bhel was a mix of puffed rice lightly roasted in some oil with finely chopped boiled potatoes and raw onions and chopped green mango. Peanuts would do as well. There had to be three chutneys, but no one could tell him what they were, though there was some speculation.

Mrs. Manly was waiting for him when he finally staggered into the kitchen and fell into a chair. She promptly handed him a glass of lemonade.

"I'm afraid I did not have much luck today, though I may have something tomorrow from Mrs. Khambatta," said William.

"That's a shame. What's it going to be for dinner, then?" Mrs. Manly asked anxiously.

"My mulligatawny soup and kedgeree."

"His favourites! That should do nicely," she said, but with a note of unease in her voice.

The captain had a vicious temper. William and Mrs. Manly had been spared the worst of it, perhaps because they were English. Spears was more severe with the Indian servants, who did not last long at Rose Hall. Nor did he have any mercy on the soldiers in the all-English unit. Captain Spears had had one too many outbursts at the British Officers' Club and was ignored when he went there, so he spent his evenings at home, drinking. Not that he drank only in the evenings. He had a strong shot of whisky right after breakfast and a couple of shots at lunch. In the evening, though, it was no-holds-barred.

Sometimes, a couple of retired old Englishmen came by to smoke, drink, and play poker with the captain. There was a lot of shouting, laughing, and banging on the table, and it usually ended with the captain showing the men his gun collection, displayed at one end of the drawing room. Spears would take out a revolver and load it, and the men would step out onto the veranda, where he would shoot a bullet into the trunk of the giant old fig tree. Then he would urge the men to try their hand, but they always declined, giving Spears the opportunity to laugh at them.

The captain would round off the evening by saying, "I won't bore you with my hunting tales again, gentlemen, but what a time I had at my old posting. Almost in the jungle we were, and come weekend, off I'd go with the raja and his entourage for a royal hunt."

As William sat down to a quick lunch, his thoughts drifted to the past. *Strange how I landed up here at Rose Hall, supervising a kitchen at an army mess that serves three meals a day to fifty soldiers from a British regiment stationed in India and putting up with a tyrant of a captain in charge.* If he had married Edwina, he wouldn't be here. When they were courting, William and Edwina met every day and were as thick as thieves for six months. Then she began to withdraw and slip away. After breaking off their engagement, she escaped to the country to tend to an ailing elderly aunt. Edwina was gone forever. *Why, why, why did she leave me?*

His best friend, Rory, had comforted him, but then the Great War broke out and Rory enlisted in the army. William was disqualified from duty due to a slight club foot, even though he walked quite normally. He had gone to the registry anyhow, and when the officer heard that he was a chef at a seafood restaurant in London, he had suggested India.

"India? Really?"

CHEF WILLIAM AND CAPTAIN TYRANT

"Why, you'll do more service feeding our troops there than by being on the front. You know, I suppose that you'd be cooking for Englishmen. There are some units there entirely made up of our people, and that's where you'd be posted," said the officer.

The recruiting officer called his colleague over, and the man was equally enthusiastic about India. William did not give his answer at once; he said he would mull it over.

"What a capital idea!" Rory said, when they met at the Drawn and Quartered that evening to enjoy a few pints. "You'll have all the fun riding the maharaja's elephants, while I get shot in some godforsaken field somewhere."

"Hush. Don't say that! It's not funny."

"Humour's all we have left, old chap."

William went back the next day and signed on. He needed to do his bit, however he could. He imagined Edwina hearing the news, having a change of heart, and flying back into his arms. Even as he got on the boat for India, he half believed that he would receive a letter from her.

Mrs. Manly broke into his reverie by bringing him a strong cup of tea, and he glanced over a week-old edition of the *Times of India*. There was no newspaper in English in Mansubh, and the Hindi newspaper was no help. Though William could have a simple conversation in Hindi, he read it poorly. Mrs. Manly hovered around.

"Why don't you improvise this dish he wants?" she asked.

"Well, I would if I could, but I don't know enough, and I don't have the main ingredient."

"Oh dear, I do hope Mr. Spears won't be too angry," said Mrs. Manly.

She went into the parlour and picked up a shawl she was crocheting. It would be her contribution to the charity bazaar at the church next week. She would also bring some light and airy sponge cakes that William would bake. Watching her, William thought, *Things have worked out quite well, all told.*

When he first arrived in Mansubh, he had been taken aback by its Englishness. The city had an Anglican church, complete with a steeple; a small public library; and a somewhat rundown theatre. The cantonment area had wide tree-lined avenues and housed the gracious Officers' Club, which had tennis courts. William had immediately taken to Rose Hall, a charming house with a well-kept garden.

After a few weeks, he discovered some of the Indian sectors in Mansubh. How different they were! The noisy, congested, colourful bazaar area with its narrow lanes, the shops cheek to jowl. The streets showcased all kinds of activities — social, religious, and commercial — not to mention stray dogs, cows, donkeys, goats, and fowl. The variety of vegetables, fruits, grains, meat, spices, snacks, and street food delighted him. He became convinced that India was the right choice for him after all.

William hired a tutor to learn the local language and started experimenting with Indian spices and ingredients. His mulligatawny soup was one of the best recipes he had developed and had been a favourite of the Knights and their guests.

Unlike the Spears, the Knights had entertained a great deal. Celeste Knight had decided that classics would reign at Rose Hall. There was always one Indian dish at each meal — be it a dal, lentils; a curry; an appetizer; or dessert. She felt a meal consisting entirely of Indian dishes was too full of contending flavours, but one dish at a time added great value.

"I never thought I'd have a London chef in my Indian kitchen," Mrs. Knight used to say.

"Pity Mansubh is not on the coast. I can't reproduce our best dishes," William told Mrs. Knight.

"You do so very much, William. Your meals are superb."

Lacking fish, William had started specializing in chicken dishes. They had their own hens at Rose Hall. A servant took care of them. William had enjoyed cooking for the Knights and creating and supervising menus for the soldiers. He got nothing but smiles from them when he made his rounds in the mess a couple of times a week. The British recruiting officers back home had been right: standard English fare was a real treat for them.

Now William started assembling the ingredients for his speciality — mulligatawny soup. It would be carrots, green peppers, onions, and chicken. He would use eggs for the kedgeree. The curry powder for the kedgeree was his own recipe. How baffled he had been by all the spices just a year ago! Now they were his best friends, and he made his own spice mixes. He had observed the head cook at the mess, then experimented and finalized his own versions.

He whistled tunelessly as he methodically chopped onions. Luckily, they did not make him cry. Hearing him, Mrs. Manly smiled. She looked forward to taking the soup and kedgeree to Mrs. Spears. Normally, she ate like a sparrow, but even she would succumb to the wonderful aromas and flavours.

I wonder what Rory is up to, thought William as he moved on to the carrots. Rory had started out in France, but it was impossible to keep up a correspondence with a soldier on the move. Since the regime change at Rose Hall four months ago, William had reread all his mother's letters, plus the few from his father and sisters. The Knights' departure had left a void.

William's one source of entertainment was a gramophone that the Knights had kindly left behind, along with a few records. He played music at a low volume. Rose Hall had thick concrete walls, but he wasn't taking any chances. Listening to the radio in the kitchen was forbidden by the captain. Mrs. Spears played the piano sometimes. She played well, and Mr. Spears permitted that, fortunately.

In his early days at Rose Hall, Edwina's image would rise before William without effort and all too frequently. But that changed as the months passed. He was going home, and back to school, as soon as the war ended. What he had earned here would pay for that education. Maybe he would get some rooms. Perhaps share with Rory? He imagined their bachelor quarters would have a small kitchen good enough for cooking up fancy brunches. They would have a night out on Friday, then sleep in. William would rise and make brunch — black currant scones with no stinting on butter; Eggs Benedict, not with bacon, but some ham that he would have cured himself; and toast with orange marmalade. They would end perhaps with a fruit salad soaked in some red wine. And there would be cups of steaming Earl Grey tea, always good for warding off the London chill. In the afternoon they would go rowing on the Thames, drifting past familiar landmarks toward the countryside. If the weather didn't hold up, they'd get a few friends together and play cards.

"He wants a whisky," said Mrs. Manly, coming into the kitchen and interrupting William's daydream.

William set up the tray with a shot of Johnnie Walker, some ice cubes, and a bowl of salted peanuts. With the Knights, he had got to show off his knowledge of punches, sours, slings, cobblers, shrubs, toddies, and flips, but when he had suggested cocktails to Spears, he had shrugged and said he liked his alcohol straight up.

The captain was sitting in his rocking chair in the living room, while Mrs. Spears sat on the sofa. She wore a pretty lilac dress, and a magazine lay open on her lap. It occurred to William for the first time that she was probably thirty years to Mr. Spears's forty.

"How's supper coming along?" asked the captain.

"Very well, sir."

"I even persuaded Miranda to come down."

"What will you have, milady?" William asked.

"A lemonade, please."

Soon the couple was seated at the dining table, the head of a sambar deer prominent on the wall behind Spears. The captain had brought it along when they moved in and got it installed right away, claiming that he had killed the beast himself.

William entered, bearing a Victorian tureen that he set down on the table.

"What's this?" asked Spears.

"Mulligatawny, sir. Mrs. Khambatta has promised the bhel recipe by tomorrow."

"What?!" the captain roared.

Henry Spears and William Harold looked at each other. The captain's eyes were bloodshot. *That's not his first drink*, William thought. *No doubt he has helped himself from the bottle in his room.* "I tried my very best, sir. I really did, but I could not find the recipe. I will make it soon, and I am looking forward to serving it."

Spears stood up. His chair fell backward, hitting the ground with a loud thud. For a moment William thought that he would strike him, but the captain stalked out of the room.

"Shall I serve you?" he asked Mrs. Spears.

Mrs. Spears shook her head and reached for a glass of water, her hand shaking a little. She made as if to take a sip, then stopped. "No, Henry, no!" she screamed.

Spears stood in the doorway, holding his revolver. As William started to turn around, the captain shot him straight through the heart. He fell forward onto the dining table. The glass in Mrs. Spears's hand fell to the floor and shattered into a thousand pieces as she slumped backward in a faint. Mrs. Manly rushed into the dining room. She froze, then burst into great, heaving sobs — inconsolable.

CHEF WILLIAM'S MULLIGATAWNY SOUP

An Anglo-Indian soup with curry powder

Vegetarian, can be vegan, gluten-free
Servings: 4-6 | Cook Time: 40 minutes | Level: Easy

INGREDIENTS

- 1-2 tablespoons butter
- 2 medium carrots, cut into ½-inch cubes
- 1 large onion, finely chopped
- 1 large sweet potato, peeled and cut into ½-inch cubes
- 1 green pepper, chopped into ½-inch pieces
- 2 medium garlic cloves, minced
- ¼–½ teaspoon salt (to taste)
- 1 apple, peeled, deseeded, and cut into ½-inch pieces
- ½–1 teaspoon Madras curry powder (to taste)
- ¼ teaspoon nutmeg powder
- 4 cups vegetable broth
- 1 tablespoon tomato paste
- ½ teaspoon black pepper powder (to taste)

For the garnish:

4 tablespoons fresh parsley, finely chopped
1-2 tablespoons natural yogurt, per serving

METHOD

1. Melt the butter in a large thick-bottomed pot on high heat and stir in the carrots, onion, sweet potato, green pepper, garlic, and salt. Cook over medium heat for about 5 minutes, stirring regularly, until the vegetables begin to soften. Stir in the apple pieces and add the curry powder and nutmeg. Cook for 1-2 minutes.
2. Add the broth and stir in the tomato paste. Add the black pepper. Bring to a boil, then reduce heat to medium and cook until vegetables are done. Check and adjust spices and salt. Remove from heat and cool a bit.
3. Use a hand mixer or a food processor to purée around ⅓ of the soup and add it back to the main container. You could also purée it all, as the texture and thickness of the soup is a personal preference.
4. Serve hot in a bowl, garnished with finely chopped parsley and a spoonful of yogurt. Keep the salt, curry powder, and black pepper handy.

NOTES

1. To make this dish vegan, use cooking oil instead of butter and skip the yogurt.

2. Madras curry powder is best, but you can use whatever curry powder you have. Always taste the curry powder to determine how hot the chili level is before adding.
3. "Mulligatawny" means "pepper water," so strong black pepper ground from peppercorn works best for this dish.

THE CRIES OF ANIMALS

Characters
King Vajradev
a sadhu, a holy man
Krishna, a Hindu god
Radha, his consort
Neminatha (Nemi), a legendary Jain teacher
Shivadevi, his mother
Rajimati, his betrothed

King Vajradev sat on a low, richly upholstered divan. Beside him was a hookah. Reclined against tasselled silk cushions, he was enjoying the pleasantly scented breeze created by two servants who stood behind him with large vetiver fans.

Seated in front of him, on a wooden bench, was a sadhu in saffron robes. Both king and holy man looked distinguished, though they exuded different kinds of power. The king wore an indulgent smile and played with the large diamond ring on his middle finger. The holy man looked severe, with his eyes fixed on the antique chessboard between them.

That morning, the holy man had appeared at the palace gate, expressing a wish to play a game of chess with the king, and was brought to Vajradev. "So, you want to leave your godly pursuits and play this lowly game with me?" Vajradev said jovially.

"Yes, and for a wager," said the sadhu.

"A wager too! What kind of a wager?"

"Oh, mighty king. If you lose, you will put a grain of rice on the first square of the chess board and double it on every subsequent one."

"There's no dearth of rice in the royal granary."

"Think carefully about what I have asked you for."

The king waved his hand in the air. "But how will you pay if you lose?" he asked.

"How I pay is my concern."

"All right, let's get started."

The game had been going on for an hour. The sadhu brought his curiously well-kept hand to an ivory chess piece. "*Shāh māt* ... checkmate," he said, half under his breath.

Vajradev's lassitude evaporated. Sitting up, he stared at the board and saw a classic checkmate, executed with the queen and a rook. There were only two things Vajradev prized as much as chess: his favourite queen and his most accomplished courtesan. He invited many to come and play with him during his off-duty hours. He rarely lost a game, and he did not like losing. Who does? Though upset, he forced a smile and sent the servants to fetch bags of rice.

On the servants' return, king and sage started counting out the grains, and an attendant deposited the exact amount into large barrels. Soon realization dawned that by the sixty-fourth square, 18,000,000,000,000,000,000 grains would be needed.

"I would say that's about two hundred and ten billion tons of rice," said the holy man. No longer serious, the sage was grinning from ear to ear.

"I've given you my word, yet I cannot keep my promise. This is very painful for me. Let us exchange our robes. You will have my kingdom, and I will enter the forest as a hermit," said Vajradev.

"Let us forget about the wager."

The king shook his head and started to take off his considerable number of jewels. Then he paused and looked keenly at the holy man. "Who are you? Who are you really?" he asked.

The sadhu smiled. The next moment, the holy man disappeared, and a handsome figure with dark blue skin was seated before the king. Clad in vermillion robes of purest silk and a jasmine garland round his neck, he wore a peacock feather in his golden crown. In his hand he held a flute that he put playfully to his lips.

"Lord Krishna!"

Leaping up from his seat, Vajradev prostrated himself before the god. The attendants followed. "Forgive me, Lord, for my foolishness. I suspected that you were not as you seemed, but then ... Please give me the chance to make amends. Please join me for lunch."

"That is a kind invitation, but I'm in a bit of a hurry," said Krishna.

"Not even the humblest guest leaves the palace without eating," Vajradev pleaded.

Krishna, a gourmet and gourmand, gave in. His earthly abode was in North India, but now he was in South India, and South Indian delicacies did not come his way easily. They proceeded to a feast of medu vadas and dal vadas, idiyappams, sambar and rasam, chettinad potato roast and bitter gourd curry, lemon rice and coconut rice, avial, vegetable stew, banana bhaji, brinjal fry, three types of papadums, six types of chutneys, four types of salad, and pickles. And, of course, there were sweet dishes — semolina fragrant with cardamom, sweet saffron rice, mysore pak, and red wheat payasam.

"I see that you are a vegetarian, like my cousin Neminatha," said Krishna.

Vajradev bowed his head. "I follow my chief queen's dictates in this regard, my lord. We have heard of Neminatha. We have heard how he was able to spin your mighty chakra that no one else can even lift. Is it true that Neminatha spun the disc around on his little finger?"

"Yes, it was so. We were just boys, playing."

"This goes to show that you do not need to eat meat to be strong," said the king.

"That is true."

"Soon, I will prepare for my departure to the forest. I must honour my word. I do not want to collect bad karma."

Krishna laid his hand on Vajradev's shoulder. "You are a just and benevolent king, yet all is not well in your kingdom. I do not want you to pay the debt directly to me. I want you to give rice to your poorest citizens. Make sure they do not go hungry. Let your heirs also practise this so that you will fulfill your wager over lifetimes."

"I will do so! I will also give everyone who comes to the Sree Krishna Swamy Ambalappuzha Temple a wonderful *prasad*, a blessed offering. The finest paal payasam in the land is made in the royal kitchen. We will serve it every day at the temple."

"I will return one day and taste this special payasam."

"Please come back soon."

"I may visit after eons, but come I will," said Krishna, smiling.

After the meal the king pressed Krishna to stay longer. They could visit the royal stables or go for a walk in the music garden. Or they could play another game.

"I actually need to hurry home for a wedding," said Krishna.

"Who is getting married?"

"It's Neminatha, in fact."

"How nice that he's getting married!"

"He didn't want to at all. It wasn't easy convincing him, but he has finally agreed. It was my wife who suggested that he marry her sister, Rajimati. A lovely, talented lady she is too. I don't know how my wife managed to convince Nemi, but she did."

"Women, they have their special ways. My chief queen can persuade me to do the very thing I have sworn not to do."

Neminatha walked stealthily through the tall, rustling wheat stalks. He could hear Krishna moving rapidly somewhere to his left. Krishna was fast, but Nemi had strategy. Nemi knew how to create a diversion by throwing a stone up high, creating rustling sounds in another part of the field, or releasing a sparrow into the wheat stalks. His many bird friends often perched on his shoulders.

Krishna was also restless and naughty. He stole the white butter churned by the *gopis* — female cowherds and milkmaids — broke their pots, and even stole their clothes when they were bathing in the river. He liked to toss stones in the river when the water rushed forward and see them rise with the swells before they were swallowed by the depths. When the river went quiet, as it did each summer, he explored the exposed bed and caught fish trapped in the shallows.

"Let them go. Why do you bother them?" Nemi would say crossly. In contrast to Krishna, Nemi liked to sit cross-legged on a large flat stone on the bank, contemplating the river, which was at times sluggish, at times in spate. He could do this for hours on end.

When Krishna entered adolescence, he got involved with an older *gopi*, Radha. He begged Nemi to look after his herd so he could go and meet her in the forest. Radha devised all sorts of stratagems to get away from her husband's household and meet Krishna. "Your cousin is rather handsome. I could introduce him to a *sakhi*, girlfriend," said Radha one day.

"Nah, waste of time. He just won't play along," said Krishna.

He had been worried that Nemi would object to his liaison with Radha and would tell on him, but Nemi seemed not to care.

"A strange one," said Radha, nodding toward Nemi.

"He's harmless enough."

Laughing, they entwined their bodies just like two young creepers, the sweet smell of Krishna's sweat sending Radha into a swoon.

Shivadevi looked at her son with pride. She was excited, nervous — Nemi was finally getting married!

Neminatha sat on a brown mare. His habitual white cotton clothes had been replaced by fine maroon linen. He had refused silk. With gold in his ears and around his neck and arms, he looked regal. The horse was also elaborately decorated for the occasion. The musicians blew into their huge sickle-shaped bugles, and the wedding procession started. The male relatives and friends led on fine horses; the women followed in covered palanquins. A line of servants came next, on foot. The marriage ceremony would take place, according to tradition, in the bride's village.

Earlier in the day, Nemi had mechanically performed the prenuptial rituals. He hated riding horses. *What made humans sit astride them and become their masters? It was a despicable idea. Why did I agree to all this?* An experienced meditator, he was trying to override his emotions, but his mind refused to be tamed. How long he sat stiffly on the horse he did not know; the ride had the hallucinatory quality of a bad dream.

Suddenly, he jerked awake from something he could not name, something he experienced as dark, gelatinous, oppressive. He came back to his senses because he heard cries, the cries of animals. There were many of them, and they were all crying piteously. The bleating of goats and the squawking of chickens filled the air.

"What's that?" he asked, turning to his uncle, who was riding a little behind him.

His uncle looked puzzled.

"The cries! Do you not hear them?"

"No, I hear nothing."

THE CRIES OF ANIMALS

How could he not hear them? Nemi wondered. The cries were loud, a cacophony rising to the skies. Then he saw the large enclosure. In separate pens there were scores of goats and chickens and dozens of deer and antelope.

"Those are the animals who will feed the guests. You know that some four hundred people will come to the feast tomorrow. Perhaps more."

An arrow pierced Neminatha's heart, the pain so sharp that he could barely breathe. As his eyes clouded with tears, the animals fell silent. When his vision cleared, he saw carcasses stretching for miles, feathers drifting in the air, the soil darkened by blood. The stench that arose from the dead, decaying beings made him gag. *That's why they had fallen silent!*

"Are you all right?" he heard his uncle ask.

The cries started up again, coming at him from all directions, from heaven above and the very bowels of the earth. Nemi pulled sharply at the reins of his horse. "Stop it!" he screamed. The mare stopped. Nemi got off and started walking stiffly to the enclosure. His lower back ached. "Please go and fetch Rajimati's father. I will wait here for him," Neminatha said to a shepherd guarding the entrance. The bearded young man trembled but hastened to do as he was told. His assistant, who remained behind, looked apprehensive.

"How many animals have been slaughtered for the feast?" Nemi demanded.

"None, sir. Not yet," said the lad. Then he looked down at his feet.

Neminatha's heartbeat slowed and his body relaxed.

Two curious goats, a male and a female, came up to the fence and looked up at Nemi. Reaching out through the slats, Nemi stroked their heads. The goats bleated, bringing a smile to Nemi's lips. *The animals called out to me and now I am here*, he thought. The procession had come to a standstill, and Nemi's uncle stood beside him.

"I was not told that there would be meat at the wedding," said Nemi evenly.

"But we did tell you. You were probably not listening. You will be served a vegetarian meal as usual."

"I see."

"What's the matter? Why have we stopped?"

Nemi said not a word. Soon Rajimati's father stood before them. Nemi bowed deeply to him. Bringing his hands together in a namaste, he said, "Sir, I'm going to do something that will grieve you deeply. I apologize with all my heart in advance. The wedding must be cancelled. I have realized that it is not possible for me to marry. I beg you to return the goats and chickens to their domestic pens and release the deer and antelope back into the forest. I know I'm hurting many people, but there is no alternative. Please ensure that not even one of these beasts is killed."

"Neminatha has broken off the wedding." The words spread like wildfire. When the news reached Rajimati's bejewelled ears, she fainted.

THE CRIES OF ANIMALS

Krishna sat across from Nemi. It was a dark, moonless night, inadequately illuminated by a single lantern placed between them. Earlier in the day, Nemi had made his declaration, swift as a thunderbolt and as consequential.

Krishna had come to see Nemi at a small hermitage at the edge of the forest, where Nemi had taken up temporary residence. It was a place Nemi knew well. Krishna was full of regret that he had come late to the wedding. He was delayed by an unexpected encounter with a demon who had to be slayed en route. He and Nemi had just started conversing. They were not just cousins but also the best of friends.

"We can serve a vegetarian meal to everyone, you know. Postpone the wedding by a couple of days. Naturally, Rajimati's father wanted to do his best for his daughter and the guests, but the killing of animals can be avoided," Krishna repeated.

"You know well that it's not just that. I cannot bear the suffering of any living being; the cruelty toward them revolts me utterly. But my real reason is much more profound. I cannot bear all the responsibilities of a house and a family, having a wife, begetting children, devoting my life to the welfare of my parents and relatives, and performing all the necessary rituals," Nemi said patiently.

"What then?"

"I will become a monk. I came before to this very hermitage and studied with the sage here. Meditated for long hours, for days. Those were the happiest times of my life. I will continue to learn from him and others. And I will develop and formulate my own ideas."

"But why this sudden change? It does not make sense."

"When I heard the animals crying, all I felt at first was great pain. It cut through me like a sword. I thought for a minute that I would die. But then I saw the great disc of the sun, spinning. And in the heart of the sun was the moon, and in the heat and beat of life, there was calm and tranquility. The image of a sage seated in meditation by the riverbank came to me. The river was in spate, but the mind of the sage was like a clear lake. Who is he? I wondered. Where have I seen that face before? And then it came to me in a flash. It was I. I was the sage, the one who gave up all worldly bonds and practised austerities. The one who renounced all. The one who gained knowledge. The one who became liberated. It was I and no other."

Krishna's voice rose, "But to what end, Nemi? You can contemplate and meditate and still live a normal life as husband and father. You must take over your father's leadership role. After all, you're his eldest son. It's your duty. To say nothing of your mother, to whom you have dealt a devastating blow."

Anguish flushed over Neminatha's face. He clasped his hands together and remained silent for a few minutes. Then his face relaxed and he said, "The end? The end is knowledge. Realization leading to liberation."

Krishna, though maintaining outward calm, was deeply disturbed. He had to argue his case with everything he had; it was his responsibility to restore Nemi to his family. He owed it to many people, most of all to Nemi himself. "Come down to earth, my friend. Do you recall how you entered the great war with me and fought on the battlefield? It was your duty as my cousin to join that righteous war when I asked you to. You never hesitated. And now you are ready to stake your whole life, and worse, on some fancy about self-realization?"

Nemi remained silent, his head bent. Krishna pressed forward.

"You got engaged to be married, and now you speak of celibacy? You gave your word, and you are going back on it? Is this not hypocrisy?"

Nemi raised his eyes, calmly meeting Krishna's gaze. "I was young when you asked for my help in battle. On the battlefield I took no life. I deflected arrows sent our way and blew your magical conch so that the terrifying sound would frighten and confuse the enemy. If you asked me to do the same now, I would refuse. I see the path I am meant to follow. It is clearly laid out before me. It would be a much greater hypocrisy to become a householder."

"And what about your betrayal of Rajimati? Isn't that dishonourable? Nobody will marry her now."

"You're right. I feel nothing but shame. I have nearly destroyed her life and brought unbearable hurt to many. Krishna, please look after her. Let her stay in your household if her father rejects or ill-treats her. Let your wife offer her all the love and care that is possible in a sisterly bond."

"And if I agree to this, what will you give me in return?"

Nemi laughed. Krishna always drove a hard bargain. "I will contemplate deeply and sincerely. I will look for a way that could help all living beings move beyond violence, beyond their karma, and become liberated."

Krishna said no more. They sat together for a while, taking in the lush beauty of the dark night and enjoying the coolness of the air, a coolness that would evaporate as the sun came up.

"Time for bed," said Krishna, smiling.

Neminatha nodded. As they looked at each other, they were transported to the open fields and pastures of their childhood, where they used to climb up a rough knoll and herd goats and cows. Krishna would sometimes play his flute, and Nemi would nod and sway to the music, perfectly content. Even though those days were long gone, they knew that their memories would always be with them, sealing their relationship, even as their futures diverged like two branches of a purposeful stream.

KING VAJRADEV'S PAAL PAYASAM

A comforting rice pudding, Indian-style

Vegetarian, gluten-free, contains nuts
Servings: 6 | Cook Time: 60 minutes, approximately | Level: Medium

INGREDIENTS

- 1¼ cups cooked white basmati rice
- 2 tablespoons ghee or coconut oil
- 2 cups milk (3½% or to taste)
- ⅓ cup sweetened condensed milk
- 2–4 tablespoons raw cashews, chopped
- 2 tablespoons raisins (optional)
- ¼ teaspoon cardamom powder (to taste)
- ¼ teaspoon clove powder (to taste)

METHOD

1. The texture of the cooked rice should be soft and mushy (see note).
2. Melt the ghee in a medium thick-bottomed pot. Add the milk and the rice. Boil on medium heat for 15 minutes, uncovered, then reduce heat to low. Mix in the condensed milk, cashews, raisins (if using), cardamom powder, and clove powder and cook for approximately 30 minutes until the mixture thickens. Stir from time to time.
3. Payasam is ready when all the milk is absorbed. Use a whisk, potato masher, or both to bring the payasam to a porridge-like consistency while still hot. Serve in a bowl, warm or chilled, sprinkled with more cardamom powder. Though not traditional, ripe raspberries or blueberries on the side add oomph and nutrition.

NOTES

1. To get the right texture for the cooked rice, start by rinsing ½ cup of uncooked basmati rice in two changes of water. Place it in a thick-bottomed pot with a well-fitting lid. Add 1¼ cups water, cover, and bring to boil. Turn the heat to low and let cook for around 15 minutes. Check to see that the rice is cooked. Once done, uncover and let the rice absorb the remaining water. Remove from heat, replace the lid, and let sit covered for 5 minutes. Fluff the rice with a fork, then cover again until ready to use. This process should

yield a bit more than 1¼ cup of soft and mushy cooked rice.
2. There are many versions of this dish. This is an easier one. Some use whole cardamom and cloves, some use coconut milk or coconut pieces, some don't use condensed milk, etc.

THE TRAVELS OF SANBUSAK

Characters
Sanbusak (San), our hero
Laleh, his mother
Ehsan, his brother
Abu Bay Haq, a Persian scholar and bureaucrat
Ferdoz, a renowned Persian poet
Yousef, a caravan leader
Walid, a camel in Yousef's caravan
Eren Kiraz, a Turkish slave
The Grand Vizier, the highest officer
Gulab, his slave
Mahmud of Ghazni, sultan of the Ghaznavid Empire
Veena, an Indian cooking teacher

HOME

"San, ey San. Sanbusak!"

Laleh's shrill voice reached him again. Sanbusak shook his head vigorously from side to side, trying to dispel the sound of his mother's voice. He was sitting by a little stream, a makeshift fishing line dangling from his hand. Rain was infrequent on the Khorasan plateau, land of the sun, yet the heavens had opened up, creating this quicksilver run of water, the afternoon sun glinting off it. It was almost a miracle.

"San!" The call was closer now, a sharp bark.

He lifted his line out of the water, sighing. If he left now, he could get away with a cuff on his ear. If he tarried, it could be a thrashing. "*Alān miyām*, I'm coming!" San yelled back. He started running, loose-limbed, toward the hut, flipping his line this way and that, pretending it was a whip keeping in check the fine horse that he was riding. Soon he was abreast with a few goats, though the goat herder was nowhere in sight. San envied the goat herder, who was only a couple of years older than him. He got to stay out all day with not a care in the world.

Laleh stood on the path halfway up the hillock where they lived, hands on hips, scowling. "Where's the firewood?"

"Firewood?"

"Yes, firewood!" Her voice rose. San remained silent. "So? You forgot?"

"I was fishing."

"Fishing? So, where are the fish?"

"I almost caught one. I was close, very close. But then you called me ..."

"Liar!"

Just then his elder brother, Ehsan, called out to them. He was a few feet away, dragging a load of sticks tied together with a piece of rope. With one leg a bit shorter than the other, he could still move at a good pace. Laleh rushed forward to help him.

Sanbusak climbed up to their hut and sat down on a large stone just outside, trailing the fishing line in the dust. He imagined that the fishing line was a leash and pictured a sandy-haired dog, like the one the goat herder had, tethered to it. Laleh and Ehsan brought the load up and leaned it against the wall of the hut. His brother, covered in sweat, smiled at him.

"Maybe you asked Ehsan to get the firewood," said San.

Laleh strode over and slapped him.

"Maamaan, let it be. Let's eat," said Ehsan.

"Tomorrow we eat fish," San declared, rubbing his cheek. *Maamaan can really deliver a good one*, he thought.

Laleh woke early the next morning. After doing her usual chores, she filled a large basket with barberries that grew wild in a thicket not far from the house and walked to the market.

It was late afternoon by the time she sold the berries. She made her way to the fortune teller at the far end of the market. The old man had spread a rug under a persimmon tree. With a canary perched on his shoulder, he sat smoking his pipe, his customers having slowed to a trickle. Laleh sat down next to his box of coloured cards as she and the fortune teller exchanged greetings. "I'm not of quiet mind," she said.

The man, looking sympathetic, waited. Laleh took her time. "It's my younger son," she said softly.

"Ah, I have seen him. A lively one."

"He's good for nothing."

"He's a child."

"He's not so young. He's fatherless and should know his responsibilities."

The man said nothing.

"Please draw a card for me," she said.

The man held out his hand and whistled to the canary, who hopped down on it. He brought it to the edge of the box, and the bird drew a card with its beak. The man read the card and said, smiling, "He's going to be a great man and travel far."

"Really?"

"The cards never lie."

"A great man how?"

"That's not clear. The boy is different. He'll find his own path."

"Will he have money? Will he be happy? Healthy?"

"Shall I pull another card?"

Laleh nodded. This time, when the fortune teller read the card, a shadow passed over his face.

"What is it?" Laleh whispered.

"It's the verse about immortality," said the fortune teller, collecting himself.

"What?"

"San will have eternal life."

"No! What do you mean? Is he a *djinn*? Oh god, what is all this?" Laleh cried out.

"Calm down, please. You misunderstand. It means that his fame, his name, will never die." He continued, "Let the boy grow as he will. I know you have only two children. It was so very tragic, your husband's death from that fall. Naturally, you worry. But San has a bright future."

Laleh's eyes filled with tears. "*Mamnoon*," she said appreciatively, clasping the old man's hand.

"Go in peace, sister. May you step lightly and may your cares fall away."

Laleh dropped a couple of coins in the dust and left.

Two years passed. San, still scatterbrained and irresponsible, turned thirteen. Laleh tried her best to knock sense into him. She even got Ehsan, the reluctant one, to give San a beating from time to time. And yet she was less anxious now, more hopeful, because the fortune teller's words kept her company.

One day a message came from her cousin who lived in the outskirts of faraway Neyshabur. He needed a helping hand, a dependable one, on his large farm. Sanbusak volunteered to go at once. This was the chance he was waiting for. His enthusiasm was infectious, and he finally convinced the skeptical Laleh. Ehsan thought it was good idea from the start. He knew that his brother was too restless to stick around their little village for long.

The day before San's departure, Ehsan got him a good luck charm from the fortune teller. It was a large glass bead with concentric circles from dark blue to light blue and then white, representing an eye. The pendant hung on a thin leather string, and it would keep San safe. Ehsan had paid the fortune teller extra to say a special prayer and make the charm foolproof.

While Ehsan was away, Laleh slaughtered a chicken. She chopped up the tender meat, then cooked it with onion, mashed chickpeas, and herbs. Squatting by the clay stove, she mixed wheat flour with water, rolling out the dough into thick rounds. She cut each circle into two equal pieces, fashioned them into triangles, and stuffed them with the meat mixture before deep-frying them in hot oil. Tears flowed as she worked.

"Stop it, Maamaan. Don't cry," said San. His excitement was tinged with sadness.

"It's the smoke from the fire, silly," said Laleh, wiping away the tears. "You're going to be a big man one day. I know."

The next day she held him for a long time before she let him go.

NEYSHABUR, PERSIA

Abu Bay Haq rose early. It was his custom to take a walk every morning and pray at the mosque before returning home to a dainty breakfast. The air was refreshingly cool when he stepped out into the garden. Stopping at the rose bushes, he regarded the perfectly shaped red buds with pleasure. By afternoon some would have bloomed, sending their heady scent into his study, where he could be found at all hours. These days the task at hand was translating a weighty manuscript from Persian into Arabic.

Bay Haq strolled down the street, pensive. He thought about how God had granted everything to Neyshabur, the city where he had recently completed his studies. It lay at the base of the splendid snow-clad Binalud Mountains, on a fertile plain spreading like a flirtatious courtesan's fan. All kinds of foodstuff flowed into the city: barley, wheat, rice; peas and lentils; mustard, garlic, onions; sesame, flax seed, herbs and spices; olives, dates, apples, persimmons, grapes, pomegranates, pears, apricots, and cucumbers; various kinds of meat; as well as wine and beer.

And yet, I won't be able to bite into those heavenly persimmons for much longer.

The city was rich in other ways. The highest-quality turquoise nestled in the heart of a mountain near Neyshabur. The serene blue stone decorated pleasure palaces and mosques alike and was used in tiles, clothing, and jewellery that travelled far and wide. The glazed ceramics made in Neyshabur were world-class, coveted in the westward cities where the *phirangis*, foreigners, lived.

Neyshabur had lovely public gardens, graceful architecture, and passionate poetic gatherings that went on all night. The roads that started from the Jade Gate in China reached Kashgar, then on they went to Samarkand, Merv, and Balkh, entering the plateau of Khorasan, land of the sun, and snaking through Neyshabur on to Rey. Caravans brought silk, tea, spices, gems, perfume, ivory, coral, glass beads, and much else. But more importantly, they brought new ideas, music, languages, and people from exotic lands. It was these riches, this exchange and intermingling, that generated an effusive bounty that sang to Bay Haq's soul.

Bay Haq was in mortal pain since he had been summoned to Ghazni, the distant capital of Sultan Mahmud, to join the monarch's secretariat there. It was a high honour, this prestigious position at such a young age, and his contemporaries were envious. And splendid it was, this Ghazni, he had heard. *Stop torturing yourself,* he told himself severely. *You've lost your heart to Neyshabur, but you must be practical. Leave you must, and so you will.*

Suddenly, a voice called out, "Watch out, sir!"

A hand grabbed his arm and pulled hard. A high neighing sound filled his ears. Looking up he saw a thoroughbred horse mounted by a soldier pass him by a hairbreadth. The sound of the hooves faded as Bay Haq lay on the ground, a cloud of dust obscuring his vision and making him cough. Someone was kneeling beside him.

"Are you hurt, sir?" It was a slight, nice-looking boy, about fifteen. Bay Haq shook his head. With the help of the boy, he was on his feet. Badly shaken, he had a few bruises but nothing serious. Bay Haq thanked Sanbusak profusely and offered him a few coins, but San refused them. He insisted on walking home with Bay Haq, then recounted his story.

"My uncle beat me every day, sir. Two long years. He gave me hardly anything to eat. I was just a beast of burden to him. No, it was worse. The cows and horses had hay and water, little treats, kind words, and strokes. He is a rich man, my uncle. We have the same blood, but I got nothing. So I ran away. I had to, sir. What else could I do?"

Sanbusak chattered on. Bay Haq wished to be rid of him, but San went on, entreating him to give him work. There was no need to pay him, he said. All he needed was a place to sleep and scraps from the dining table. And so, San joined Bay Haq's household as a servant he did not need.

Alas, San was unfit for the vocation. Some mornings he would sleep in after being out late, even though it was his job to serve Bay Haq breakfast. When they sent him to the market, he got engrossed in watching the cock fights instead of hurrying home with the supplies. When they asked him to clean the house, he broke a precious vase.

There was one and only one area where he showed some talent and application — cooking. After he had learnt some basics from Bay Haq's cook, San started making suggestions about adding or subtracting a condiment, which would always improve the original recipe. How about a bit more lime juice or a hint of tahini, a teaspoon of rosewater, or a few pinches of cinnamon? Why not replace the rosewater with saffron, eliminate the cumin in this one, he would say. However, San's apprenticeship as a cook was also short-lived. San lost interest in the kitchen and started making all kinds of mistakes. The exasperated cook took his complaints to Bay Haq.

"Don't worry," said Bay Haq. "San won't be accompanying us to Ghazni, though he has begged me to take him along. I have told him that his work with us ends when we leave Neyshabur."

The cook turned away with a sigh of relief.

DESERT NIGHT

Sanbusak sat by the campfire while his travelling companions lay curled up in blankets around him, dozing. He, too, was wrapped in a heavy wool blanket that the *madouga*, caravan leader, Yousef, had given him. Despite being let go by Bay Haq in Neyshabur, Sanbusak had decided to follow him.

San had never experienced the all-consuming cold of desert nights. It took over his body, stunning the mind, eliminating all other sensations and thoughts. Only a deep, pure experience of frigidity remained. And it was summer! Nevertheless, bit by bit, during those four weeks on the road, he got used to it. They were now a little more than halfway through their journey, and he came to dread the blistering hot days more. Often, they rested during the hottest hours, walking at night, guided by the stars.

Camels and humans walked together. At times a man would climb onto a camel's back and bump along for a few hours, but usually everyone just walked. Frequently restless and questing, San had come to love the spacious silence, the sense of simple peace and purpose that enveloped camel and man as they put one foot after another. The act of walking together had become a ritual.

The men in the group prayed five times a day. Sometimes these merchants visited a mosque in the towns where they stopped. San did not go, for he was Zoroastrian. Not that he took any particular comfort from the faith he was born into. Sometimes the men broke out into full-throated singing in Arabic. San did not join in, though he found the rough voices reverberating in unison invigorating. He would have been more comfortable singing in Dari, his mother tongue. The men often sang a song about how humans have always walked, walked long, walked hard — crossing savannah, desert, and mountain — and how this memory of walking ran through human limbs. A memory they would carry with them into paradise.

While the dusty towns they passed through held some interest for San, it was the nights they spent under the vast inky sky that thrilled him beyond measure. He could not get enough of that spare landscape of undulating sand dunes, illuminated by a cool white light or plunged into gloom. The desert was as infinite as the star-speckled heavens that stretched above.

If only he could tell Maamaan and Ehsan about his latest adventure. He imagined sitting at a fire like this one, encircled by the entire village, with everyone listening, rapt and full of admiration, some filled with envy. Even the village headman deferred to him, keeping his old white-crowned head bowed.

The decision to go to Ghazni was easy enough, but it was not obvious how San would finance his journey. Bay Haq had given him some money to help him until he found other work, but San spent it all on gambling and brothels. Left without funds, San went to his uncle, who had disowned him so vehemently, even though he had given Bay Haq a different story. There he had spun a new yarn. Instead of speaking in their mother tongue, San employed the mellifluous Farsi he had learned in Bay Haq's household. His uncle finally gave him money and said, "Don't ever show me your face again. You understand? I will set the dogs after you, and I mean it."

Thus, San was able to pay Yousef for a spot in the caravan. He had charmed him with wild tales in street Arabic, stories he had picked up from hanging around in the market, gambling dens, and whorehouses. He enjoyed salting and peppering them. Yousef had been amused enough to lend

San the life-saving blanket, which he now wrapped himself in as he sat mesmerized by the dying embers of the fire, a spot of heat in the blazing cold. He lay down, feeling suddenly tired. *Well, I did manage to come this far*, he thought. *Soon we will reach Ghazni. Who knows, perhaps I will see Sultan Mahmud's palace?*

Early the next morning, he was rudely woken up by shouts and clanging bowls. This was how Yousef set the twelve-camel caravan in motion. San leapt to his feet. He saw that the camels were already loaded and roped head to tail. The company was ready to go. Throwing the blanket over his shoulder like an awkward shawl, he started walking abreast of the third camel. They had not gone very far when Walid, the oldest camel — a massive ungainly beast with the worst breath of the lot — tottered and collapsed. Bundles of salt, wheat, and wool tied to his flanks and back went down with him, but they did not burst or break free.

"*Ya ibn el kalb* ... son of a dog!" cried Yousef.

From the beginning of the journey, Walid's health was a much-discussed topic. There was no consensus on whether they should have brought him along, whether to sell him in the next town and buy another camel, whether to abandon him on the road, or whether to just keep going. En route, Yousef pointed out the bones of dead camels to Sanbusak. Camels, though very precious, had to be let go at times. Now Yousef examined Walid closely with three other members of the caravan while San hovered around anxiously.

"He is not dead, by the grace of God. He has opened his eyes, but will he be able to get up, to walk?" asked Yousef. Opinions differed. While the four men debated, Walid was offered hay and water.

"Offer him some dates; he really likes them," said San. No one acted on his suggestion. Luckily, Walid revived and they made it to the next town, where a camel trader took him off their hands and paid Yousef a decent sum. Yousef went looking for a replacement, and the men dispersed after deciding that they would all meet up again in a couple of hours.

"Goodbye, Walid," said San softly, giving him an affectionate pat and a handful of dates. The animal devoured them, fixing his large watery eyes on Sanbusak. San could have sworn that he looked grateful.

A MEETING OF LIKE SOULS

Bay Haq was deep in conversation with Ferdoz, a famous poet who hailed from the Khorasan region. They were sitting in Bay Haq's well-appointed salon, in his spacious house in Ghazni. From time to time, Bay Haq drew languidly on the water pipe beside him. Ferdoz, curiously, abstained from smoking and drinking.

Apart from this peccadillo, there was much to admire and enjoy about Ferdoz, not least his eloquent Farsi. Since moving to Ghazni, Bay Haq was subjected far too frequently to the harsher notes of Arabic. Not that there was any dearth of Farsi speakers in town; Sultan Mahmud's court was rife with them. But there could be no sweeter experience for Bay Haq than speaking to Ferdoz in their mother tongue, the lilt peculiar to Khorasan reverberating through the air. As they freely exchanged ideas, they tackled serious topics, joked, reminisced, and segued into poetry recitation, in no seeming order.

"I met San on my way in," said Ferdoz. "What a character! He held forth on the homing pigeons that are trained at the royal *kabutarkhana*. His knowledge of the subject is impressive."

Bay Haq shrugged.

"I know you don't think well of him, but ..." said Ferdoz.

"He's a charmer, intelligent and curious. I taught him chess in Neyshabur, and just a few weeks later, he almost defeated me. But then he lost interest, and that was that. Any sustained effort seems contrary to his nature."

"Chess? Really? Anyhow, I've been thinking ... perhaps he should be introduced at the palace? In fact he hinted that he would like to work there."

"Take him, take him! You'll be doing us a great favour."

"Why, really!"

The two friends started laughing.

"But there is one thing. If there is any trouble, you must take responsibility," said Bay Haq, only half serious.

"I pledge to do so," Ferdoz responded solemnly.

Soon they were at the table, partaking in a lovely meal composed of typical dishes served at refined tables in

Khorasan. But there was a surprise — it came in the form of little triangular pastries with a thin, crisp, light brown skin. Ferdoz had tasted them at street corners back home, a crude little snack made of minced meat with a couple of herbs mixed in. But here the pastry was transformed! There was minced meat but also nuts and dry fruits, finely chopped. The blend of meat, nuts, and dry fruits with spices and herbs was nothing short of masterful. The aroma was delightful, the taste sublime.

"What is this?" he asked.

"Why, it is our very own sanbusak," said Bay Haq, smiling. "Believe it or not, our shiftless San has a way in the kitchen."

"Well, perhaps he will fit in well in the royal kitchen."

"Perhaps. But my friend, you need to be careful. It seems that you are rather at odds with Sultan Mahmud. I am happy that your incomparable poem, "Shahnameh, The Book of Kings," caught the sultan's fancy, and you are an honoured guest-poet at his court. Another feather in the sultan's crown. But the couplets you wrote lately in praise of Mahmud are rather pallid, I hear."

Waving his hand dismissively, Ferdoz focused on the sanbusak.

"No, seriously, I hear Mahmud is displeased to the extent that your days at court may be numbered?"

Ferdoz stopped eating and looked squarely at Bay Haq. "Like you, I am Persian. And I am Shia. I must be true to my roots and traditions. And who is Mahmud? A Turkish pagan, an opportunist who converted to Sunni Islam and threw in his lot with the Arabs. Yes, he's the most powerful ruler ever produced by the Ghaznavid dynasty, with his ever-expanding kingdom, but what of that? Must I bow down to such a man? Or do I have a choice?"

"Say no more. The walls have ears. I know you're focused on a great work on the former glory of Persia, and that is as it should be. But why compromise on the verses you wrote for the sultan? Living only in the past will get us nowhere. In any case, Mahmud does not dismiss Persia but seeks a comingling of Persian and Arabic styles."

Ferdoz shrugged. Smiling, he said, "You do well, Bay Haq, by committing to write a splendid history of Mahmud's dynasty. Each must follow his own path, and all are true, so long as you delve deep into scholarship and artistry. As for me, I find it hard to trample upon my soul and serve a master who is perhaps unworthy."

After the departure of his satiated guest, Bay Haq took a stroll in his garden. He had insisted that the gardener grow roses, even in the hardy climate of Ghazni. He simply could not do without them. The rose bushes took him back to Neyshabur and his first meeting with San. Then he recalled how San had caused havoc in the household with his negligent attitude. So why had he taken San in again, at Ghazni? Bay Haq retained a hazy memory of the morning, a year ago, when San had forced his way into his study and spoken at length, cajoling and convincing. *If Ferdoz introduces him in the palace, we'll be rid of him*, he thought. *But how long will Ferdoz last?* He was worried for him.

While he would always love Neyshabur, Bay Haq had adjusted well to Ghazni. His position was secure, and he had risen in the ranks since his arrival. His chief delight was the sultan's growing library. Bay Haq spent long hours among the wonderful volumes. He could send emissaries throughout Mahmud's vast empire to procure books he had heard about. How strange and contrary this sultan could be: a ruthless, violent plunderer abroad, particularly in the eastern lands of the heathens, yet an immaculate patron of the arts at home.

Haq looked up at the vast sky speckled with subdued stars. The moon was more than half full and luminous. He remembered lines from a couplet about the much-celebrated orb and the beauty of women, something about the fullness of time and the inevitability of death. Stepping inside, he went to bed and fell into an uneasy slumber.

PALACE DREAM

Eren Kiraz sat in the kitchen, frying triangular pastries in oil. He was not alone in this task. The head cook had organized an assembly line. There were young men rolling out the pastry; others filling it with a fragrant mixture of minced meat, onion, nuts, dry fruits, and spices; and yet others, like Eren, frying the sanbusak.

Eren wished San was working beside him, but he was at the other end of the line, stuffing the pastries. The young Persian had recently joined the royal kitchen, and his name was a constant source of derision for some. Imagine being named after a pastry! But San had a knack for improving recipes, which brought him to the head cook's notice. The kitchen staff threw barbs at Sanbusak, viewing him as a usurper getting ahead through charm and deceit, not hard work and loyalty. The new entrant neither cared nor pretended to, but soft-hearted Eren felt sorry for him. A Turkish slave brought to Ghazni two years ago and put to work in the royal kitchen, Eren had become San's friend.

That night, Sultan Mahmud was entertaining fifty guests in the great hall of his marble palace. Men sat on thick, intricately woven rugs in circles of five or six around low tables, grouped by rank and profession. Each table would be served a surfeit of dishes on large metal plates, and the distinguished company would break bread together, wine flowing like water, since water was more scarce than wine in that parched land. Looking down from its vantage point well above sea level, Ghazni reigned supreme, with no other city to rival it for hundreds of miles.

Mahmud's drinking parties were as numerous as his military forays. The conquering Sultan was forever on a march. When he came home, he teetered between devout worship — fasting and praying five times or more a day — and bouts of dissolute drinking. He could outdrink all the noblemen, military men, administrators, traders, artists, and visitors at his court. Or did diplomacy and fear compel them to pretend that the sultan could hold his liquor better than them?

San filled pastry after pastry, unmindful of what he was doing, then sealed each sanbusak with a bit of water. He was physically present, but his mind, heart, and soul dwelt in the grand vizier's mansion just outside the palace precincts. Gulab, his beloved, lived there. Gulab was named after a flower, the best flower of them all — the rose. All other people had ceased to exist; everything else was shadow. The ornamented palace that had so dazzled San when he first got here was now a mere backdrop. Gulab's image dominated the space.

San could not envision that he would ever gain the attention of the vizier's favourite slave and concubine, who was from the eastward lands of the heathens. San had first seen Gulab in the market, buying a bolt of fine, pale blue silk. His tall, slim, and graceful figure, languid eyes, fine brow, and expressive mouth had entranced San. He followed him to the vizier's residence and, after much waiting, spied on him again through a window of the music room. Sitting in that large airy room and accompanied by a lute player, Gulab sang in a high, sweet voice, his lips slightly parted, one hand raised in the air, his eyes solemn. Through the window, Gulab smiled at San, throwing coy glances his way. Or was it a fantasy conjured up by San's fevered brain?

"Watch where you're going!"

San was brought into the present; he had narrowly missed a collision with another server. Forcing himself to concentrate, he carried a platter laden with food to one of the tables in the great hall. He thought of Bay Haq. Since he could not spot him among the notables he was serving, he was probably sitting at the other end of the room. San used to drop by his former master's house from time to time, and Bay Haq occasionally sought him out in the royal kitchen, but they had not met recently. The pursuit of his beloved left San with no time for anything else. Oh, the folly of first love!

San's obsession had not gone unnoticed. "You mad? Do you have a death wish? Come to your senses, San!" Eren admonished him. The head cook threatened to get him sacked, but Sanbusak paid no heed. *It can't be long now till he gets caught*, Eren thought, as he watched anxiously from the sidelines. Should he go to Bay Haq and tell him what was going on? Beg him to knock some sense into San?

BANISHED

When Sanbusak came to, he was lying on a mud floor. It was pitch dark. He ached all over, and his left cheek felt sore. He touched a raw wound and flinched. He licked his fingers, tasting salty blood. His head felt heavy, oh so heavy. He slowly tried to sit up. Pain, he was in such pain!

Wincing, he fell back to the floor. Hazy memories appeared. The beating, being dragged to the makeshift prison behind the mosque. Gulab! He remembered it all now. They had caught him on the balcony leading to Gulab's chamber. He had managed to climb a tree and make a daring leap from a branch to the railing. A young servant girl had seen him. Stifling a scream, she ran to inform the guards about the intruder.

San stared into the void. *They will never, never, let me near him*, he thought. *They will kill me rather than have me see him again. It's all for good. I hope they kill me soon. Tomorrow, yes, tomorrow would be a good day to die.*

He noticed that the pendant his brother had given him was gone. He had worn it all through the years, restringing it as needed. The image of his mother squatting by the clay stove, making flatbread, flashed through his mind. He could not see her face, but his eyes followed the movement of her hands. There was always fresh flat bread at home. He felt tears welling up and a few trickled down his cheeks.

"Let them spare my life. I have strayed too far from home," he said, startled by the sound of his hoarse voice. He sat down, his back to the cold stone wall, and started praying — he who never prayed. He told Ahura Mazdā, God, that he wanted to return to his family; he begged to be saved.

As dawn broke over the city and before news of San's foolishness became the talk of the town, Eren went to see Bay Haq. Bay Haq agreed at once to go the vizier and plead on behalf of Sanbusak.

"He is too brazen to be made a good slave. So banishment it must be and death if he ever returns," pronounced the vizier.

The vizier wanted to sentence San to fifty lashes, but Bay Haq, speaking with great eloquence, persuaded the vizier to reduce the beating to thirty.

A crowd assembled to watch the spectacle, among them Eren. As the whip whistled through the air landing on his bare back again and again, San made no sound. He was unseeing, deaf, indifferent to the world. Eren wept, looking away. Some of the men rejoiced and jeered through the flogging, but most watched in silence.

San left town ignobly, sitting slumped forward on a donkey, eyes dull and vacant. He moved in the opposite direction from the little village where he had been born, away from the Khorasan plateau, land of the sun, and Neyshabur, city of turquoise, finest in the world. Eren followed the donkey caravan to the end of town and watched it head east — away from Ghazni, Mahmud's great capital — until it was a speck, a speck that finally dissolved into the distance.

As San left town, Bay Haq sat in his study, still as a pillar. He longed for his waterpipe but could not summon up the energy to call for the servant. Just a few weeks ago, Ferdoz had left the sultan's court of his own will and returned to Neyshabur. Now San was gone. Only the faithful old cook remained.

The roses in the garden just outside the study bloomed and sent a trail of scent toward their master. Bay Haq awoke from his reverie. He had an important appointment for which he could not afford to be late. He paused at a rose bush in the garden. Plucking a white rosebud, he tucked it into the buttonhole of his jacket. *I wear a red rose for festive occasions, so why not a white one to mark a tragedy or two?* he thought.

NOMADIC

San rolls the dice in his left hand and throws them onto the low table, where he is sitting in the company of three other men.

His eyes sparkle as he sees six plus six, twelve. He has won again. But soon his winning streak turns on him, and he ends up losing quite a bit of money. He promises to repay it the following night. He leaves his companions with a *salaam* and a smile. He knows that he will never see them again.

Forty-three years have passed since San's exile from Ghazni. Every hair on San's head is the same shade of dark brown as on the day he was born. His light brown skin is still smooth, his gait that of a man in his early forties, his mind fresh and sharp. He lives in Lahore, a city within the purview of the Ghaznavid Empire, a city Bay Haq would have liked, for culture and learning thrive here. Establishing himself as a small trader in Lahore, San has taken a wife, an older woman of some substance, and his best friend, a sea-faring merchant, is his long-time lover. Both wife and lover have aged.

Early the next morning, long before the city awakens, San rides away on a good horse, carrying small valuables and some clothes, all packed in two large leather saddlebags. He also has a pouch with gold coins in the inner pocket of his jacket. His heart is heavy, but his mind is clear, his eyes focused on the road ahead. During the long, tiring ride, the image of Gulab — sitting in the music room, his lips slightly parted, one hand raised in the air, his eyes solemn — surfaces in San's mind, then fades away. After many miles he is forced to stop to rest his horse and provide him with some fodder and water.

Sanbusak's next stop is the holy city of Kashi, located on the banks of the river Ganges. He lives here and trades, making some friends but keeping the bonds light. Every thirty years or so, he moves, taking with him his monstrous secret. He has his beloved cities. He lives in Delhi during Mughal rule, where Persian culture and cuisine are ascendent, mixing with other influences. He loves beautiful, dusty Rajasthan, particularly Jaisalmer, a town at the edge of the Thar Desert. He walks again through arid soil, over high mountains, a trader carrying his goods with a caravan of donkeys. He leaves Jaisalmer and goes to the other end of the trail. Taraz, in central Asia, is yet another ancient city located on the Silk Road. He also calls the Levant and eastern and southern Africa home for a few centuries.

Yet he is afraid to go back to Neyshabur, to the Khorasan plateau. He does not know why, but he keeps away. Finally, in the early 1700s — skirting Ghazni, the city from which he was once banned — he returns to the fabled city of turquoise, but he has come too late. Expecting a sense of kinship, he feels nothing. Worse, he feels indifferent, apathetic. Even the image of Gulab, which he has clung to for all this time, is losing its contours, slipping away. He makes his way to an opium den and stays in that quarter for weeks. Shaking off his all-too-distant past, burying misty memories of Gulab, Bay Haq, Laleh, Ehsan, and Ferdoz, he heads resolutely into the future.

Everywhere he goes, he goes alone, carrying his terrible secret. Cycling through professions, people, and moods, solitude becomes a habit. Yet more than anything, he longs to tell his story to a healer, a saint, a wise man, anyone who may be able to explain what's going on. Anyone who might be able to help him. He thirsts for a cure. He wishes for an end. But he is too afraid to turn to anyone, his undying youth a curse. He knows that the world is a dangerous place for a freak who is exposed.

Everywhere he goes, he meets his namesake — sanbusak, the pastry, in its many manifestations: The perky classic Indian samosa, with potatoes, chickpeas, and garam masala, served with a chutney. The samsa, replete with delicious fruity jams or with toasted ground almonds and sugar, flavoured with cinnamon and orange blossom water. The moon-shaped sambusak, dotted with poppy or sesame seeds, fattened with a cheese and parsley filling. The samoosa, stuffed with ground beef and spiced up with curry powder. Once he even encounters a samousa soup, leftover samousas chopped up and immersed in a spicy lentil soup.

Insatiable is the appetite for these convenient triangles. They are to be found in all kinds of eateries and homes, ranging from the humblest to the most opulent. Dingy little shops and fancy stores all carry them. As the twenty-first century kicks off, they even make their way into super lit supermarkets. They are ever-present — beloved, coveted, irresistible — devoured by one and all.

PRESENT-DAY MONTREAL

His skin tone is a pleasing light brown. Age indeterminate. Almond-shaped eyes, dark brown, and a crewcut. Square jaw, even teeth, nice smile.

When he volunteers to chop onions, I notice the beautiful turquoise bracelet on his wrist. He is the only man in my class that day. The three female students, middle-aged, amicable, seem drawn to his exotic presence, sometimes casting him sidelong glances.

He has not yet paid for my Fun with Baked Samosas Indian cooking class. He called at the last minute and said that his computer had broken down, so he could not send an e-transfer. Could he still come, please? He was so very sorry, and he would bring cash. I agreed. Curious about his accent, I asked him about his origins.

He tells me that he is from Iran. I know a few first-generation Iranian immigrants, and this is not a typical accent. When he tells me his name I ask, "Really? Samosa?"

"Yes," he says, laughing, and I join in.

Later on, we all sit around my dining table, eating the fruits of our labour: The standard potato samosa from North India, which has gone global, and a samosa from Maharashtra, my home state in India, known locally as karanji. It is stuffed with peas seasoned with fried spices, coconut, and a special spice mix called goda masala. We also make a sour, tongue-tickling tamarind chutney that is always a hit. I mention how these baked samosas are healthy, yet so flavourful, and vegan too.

"So, what do you think?" I ask him.

"Good. Very good. Never eaten this kind of samosa before, the one with peas."

I explain how there is also a sweet version of karanjis in Maharashtra, stuffed with sweetened coconut, fresh or desiccated, and flavoured with cardamom, queen of spices.

"I have eaten sweet samosas, but not those ones," says San.

"Sweet samosas? Where?"

"Uzbekistan."

I am jealous. I have always wanted to go to central Asia to see those fabled cities on the ancient Silk Road. "Ladies, we have the real McCoy here," I say suddenly, my tone dramatic. "What I mean is that we have the namesake of the samosa! The samosa very likely originated in Persia, and sanbusak was one of the names it was called in those early days. Perhaps you have a story to tell," I say to San.

"I sure do," he responds, with an easy smile.

The women leave soon after, but San lingers. We chat over cups of masala chai. As he prepares to leave, he writes me a cheque. I am unsurprised when it bounces. Normally, I would be furious, but this time I do not mind. He is a bullshitter through and through, but he had given me the recipe for the tempting fruit jam–filled samsa from Uzbekistan and entertained me for hours with incredible yarns. It was a fair deal.

VEENA'S KARANJIS

Subtly spiced baked peas-and-coconut samosas

Vegan, gluten-free

Servings: 16 medium-sized karanjis | Cook time: 1½ hours |
Level: Medium to Difficult

INGREDIENTS

- 1½ tablespoons cooking oil
- 1 teaspoon cumin seeds
- 1 teaspoon black mustard seeds
- ½ teaspoon turmeric powder
- pinch of asafoetida
- ½ cup desiccated unsweetened coconut
- 3 cups frozen green peas, defrosted
- 2 teaspoons goda masala (recipe on page 37)
- ½ hot green chili, finely chopped
- 1–1½ teaspoons black pepper (to taste)
- ½ teaspoon salt (to taste)
- 1 tablespoon lemon juice (to taste)
- 2 frozen puff pastry sheets, roughly ½ pound each, defrosted as per package instructions

METHOD

1. Line two baking trays with foil. Set aside.
2. For the vegetable filling, place a thick-bottomed pot on the stove and put the heat on medium-high. Add oil. After 30 seconds, add the cumin seeds, mustard seeds, turmeric powder, and asafoetida. When the spices start sizzling and become fragrant, reduce heat to medium-low and add the coconut.
3. Fry, stirring well with a wooden spoon, until the coconut starts browning lightly and turns fragrant. Add 1–2 tablespoons of water if needed to prevent sticking.
4. Add the peas and mix well. Also add the goda masala, chili, black pepper, and salt. Mix well and let cook for 10 minutes on low heat. Remove from heat.
5. Add lemon juice. Taste and adjust the spices (goda masala, chili, black pepper, salt). Do not add more of the fried spices. The mixture should be savoury rather than spicy.
6. Preheat oven to 375°F.
7. Dust a chopping board with some flour and place a puff pastry sheet on it. Use a rolling pin to thin out the sheet a little bit. Cut into rounds about 4–5 inches in diameter.
8. Fill half the round with a heaped tablespoon of the vegetable mixture and fold over to make a semicircular turnover. Seal the edges firmly by pressing down on them. Use a bit of water if necessary. Place on a baking tray.
9. Some scraps of pastry dough will remain after

you've made around 6–7 karanjis with one pastry sheet. Knead the scraps into a ball, then roll it out with a rolling pin and make the final karanjis in whatever shape possible. Repeat with the second sheet.

10. Once the karanjis are all assembled and lined up on the baking trays, brush both sides of each pastry with oil, ideally with a basting brush, and bake for around 20 minutes or until they are a light brown, turning them after 10 minutes.
11. Serve warm with spicy ketchup. You can spice up normal ketchup by adding sriracha, a hot sauce.

NOTES

1. Indian cooking needs a cooking oil with a high-smoke point, such as sunflower, vegetable, or canola oil.
2. Asafoetida can be bought whole in some natural food stores or online, then crushed into a powder. It can also be bought as a powder at Indian stores, but often contains additives, including wheat. Be sure to look for a gluten-free version if there are allergy concerns.
3. Karanjis are traditionally deep-fried, but I prefer them baked. They are healthier and just as delicious.
4. I use puff pastry sheets to save time. You can use a cookie cutter to cut out even circles, but the sharp edge of a metal container will also work well.
5. Karanjis stay well in the fridge for 2–3 days. When reheating, use a toaster oven rather than a microwave.

AFTERWORD

HOW THIS BOOK CAME TO BE

In 2015, for a host of reasons, I started giving Indian vegetarian cooking classes. My lifelong passion for writing and reading also led me to seek out captivating fictional narratives about food. It was then that I encountered the legend of Annapurna, the Indian Goddess of Nourishment.

Given the centrality of food in human life, there are many myths, legends, folktales, and historical narratives across cultures that are connected to food in one way or another. The Indian subcontinent offered much inspiration.

As I discovered or rediscovered these food-related tales, I started reimaging them as literary fiction. I believed that this could lead to more interesting, nuanced, complex stories that would hold greater appeal for the contemporary reader. I also decided to include one recipe per story, attributing it to a character, and in two instances, to a food ingredient.

I used beloved stories I had encountered as a child — like those of the Moghul Emperor, Akbar, and his clever courtier, Birbal. As an adult who turned toward Buddhism, I found the Buddhist parable "Three Grains of Mustard" very appealing. While Zoroastrians (later known as Parsis) fleeing religious prosecution in antiquity is a fact, I also knew a food legend associated with what happened when they landed in India. A folktale featuring the resourceful Parvati bai came to me via a storyteller friend. Some legends and historical narratives were mere slivers. Other stories, like "The Travels of Sanbusak," are entirely imaginary. All the stories involved research.

In writing *Annapurna's Bounty*, I wished to create an optimistic and enjoyable work, which also had some depth. Amen.

MORE INFORMATION ON SOME OF THE STORIES

Interlude

This section talks about food in the ancient Harappan/Indus Valley civilization (3300 BCE to 1300 BCE). Contemporary to ancient civilizations in Egypt, Mesopotamia, and China, Indus Valley was a Bronze Age civilization that is the oldest in the Indian subcontinent and among the oldest in the world. From west to east, Indus Valley spread across modern-day Afghanistan, Pakistan, and India. The ruins are still being excavated, and you can visit some of the excavation sites. The site called Farmana — near modern-day Delhi, India's capital — is mentioned in the interlude.

The town planning in Indus Valley, with symmetric streets and indoor water and drainage systems, feels modern. Indus Valley was a very urban civilization. What's more, the civilizations that arose in India after Indus Valley exhibit very different features, making this particular civilization unique and distinct. There are many unknowns about this civilization, as the Indus Valley script has not yet been deciphered. Still, historians have quite a lot to say about Indus Valley.

The society may have been relatively egalitarian, as there is no evidence of monumental buildings, like palaces. Also striking is the near absence of obvious places of worship or idols (i.e., gods). This was a very organized society, with standard weights and measures in use. It covered a large area and supported substantial populations. Apart from residential structures, the buildings found or reconstructed include granaries and bathhouses, a citadel in Harappa, a fortified city, and a port in Lothal. While Harappa and Mohenjo-Daro, which is the other great Indus Valley city, are in modern-day Pakistan, Lothal is in India.

A word about the river Indus. Called Sindhu in Sanskrit, an ancient Indian language, this great river is approximately 3,180 kilometres long and flows from west to east across Pakistan, northern India, and western Tibet.

Do the Right Thing

This story features Guru Nanak (1469–1539) as one of the characters. He was the founder of Sikhism, a religion that originated in the Indian subcontinent. The story mentions community kitchens called *langars*, which can be found in all *gurdwaras* (i.e., Sikh places of worship), everywhere in the world.

A *langar* is inside or attached to a *gurdwara* and serves simple, free, and nutritious meals to anyone who goes there, no matter what their background. The concept of the *langar* is central to Sikhism and it was introduced by Guru Nanak.

You can read more about *langars* as a concept, as well as *langars* in Canada and elsewhere, in the interesting academic article "Food That Builds Community: The Sikh *Langar* in Canada" by Michel Desjardins and Ellen Desjardins (erudit.org/en/journals/cuizine/1900-v1-n1-cuizine3336/037851ar/). Here is an illustrative quote from the article: "Inspired by contemporary Sufi practice, as well as by Guru Nanak's concern for feeding the poor and removing divisions between people, the *langar* blossomed in the early decades of the emergence of this new religious movement. By the early 17th century it had become a Sikh fixture, and the practice continues to this day."

The Cries of Animals

This story features a Hindu holy man, who turns out to be Lord Krishna in disguise, asking a king to donate rice to his subjects. The king agrees. As well, says the king, he would serve paal payasam (Indian rice pudding), every day, to the devotees who come to a Hindu temple, devoted to Lord Krishna. Further, he promises Lord Krishna that future generations of his family will continue these practices.

In India, at times legends do not remain in the past; they continue into the present. Below, I give you the continuation of "The Cries of Animals":

Many are the grand and rich temples in India; their architecture, artistry, and antiquity can take your breath away. The Sree Krishna Swamy Ambalappuzha Temple is chaste in comparison but nevertheless large and impressive. Built in the traditional, local style, the cluster of buildings have steeply sloped red-tiled roofs and white-washed walls. Dedicated to Lord Krishna and located in the verdant coastal state of Kerala, this temple is situated on a lake.

People come here not just to worship or sightsee; they are also drawn by taste, flavour, and aroma. Every day the temple serves "the most delicious paal payasam in the world." This Indian rice pudding, made with rich, frothy, high-quality cow's milk, fragrant with ghee, is slow-cooked with cardamom.

First offered to the gods and sanctified, this blessed *prasad* is then enjoyed by all, for a price. It comes in two sizes. Was there always a price tag, I wonder. It is unlikely, as *prasad* is traditionally offered in temples free of charge. Perhaps the expensive ingredients, and the number of people drawn to the temple to savour the famous paal payasam, warrant the price? In any case, the paal payasam is served every day, and the king's delicious promise to Lord Krishna continues to be fulfilled!

A FINAL WORD ON INDIAN COOKING

There is often room in Indian cooking for the cook to modify a recipe based on their tolerance for heat or their preference for certain spices. I invite you to experiment, adding more or less spice, as you desire. But remember, when adding extra spices at the end of a recipe, add only those that were introduced later in the process, not those that were fried at the start. You can also place spice mixes or chili powder on the dining table to let people add more of these to their own plate as they want. In India, this is not considered an insult to the cook. Enjoy!

ACKNOWLEDGEMENTS

Every work of fiction is a collective endeavour.

Thanks are due to Taima Tyebjee, Qaid Silk, Mandira Kumar, Hutokshi Doctor, and Khosro Berahmandi for variously contributing to this project.

Clare Thorbes, Mark Frutkin, Aparna Kaji Shah, Nilambri Ghai, Loredana Monte, Caroline Connell, my mother Pramil, my brother Amar, Sue Zelinksi, Gillian Kranias, Greg Lynch, Sarah Giddens, Shernaz Kennedy, Himmat Singh Shinhat, and Diane Opala all gave valuable feedback.

Diversité artistique Montréal, Festival Accès Asie (Montreal), Festival des traditions du monde de Sherbrooke, and the Women's Art Society of Montreal supported storytelling based on some of the legends.

I am very grateful to my partner, Marc-Antoine Parent, who carefully read the manuscript and helped me improve it.

A huge thank you to Julia Kim, who championed and edited the book. It was wonderful to work with her. Many thanks to all the Dundurn staff that I worked with, including Janna Green, the copy editor. Erin Pinksen, who edited the recipes and oversaw the editorial process, deserves a special mention. *Merci.*

Last, but certainly not least, *merci beaucoup* le Conseil des arts et des lettres du Québec for a generous writing grant.

ABOUT THE AUTHOR

VEENA GOKHALE, an immigrant shape-shifter, started her career as a print journalist in Bombay. This tough, tantalizing city inspired her book, *Bombay Wali and Other Stories* (Guernica Editions, 2013). Veena first came to Canada on a journalism fellowship and returned to do a masters. Then she started working with non-profits. Her novel, *Land for Fatimah* (Guernica Editions, 2018), is partly inspired by a two-year stint with an NGO in Tanzania.

After following her French-Canadian partner to Montreal, Veena started learning French and teaching vegetarian Indian cooking classes. She sought food-related legends and did some storytelling around them at multicultural events. This led to *Annapurna's Bounty: Indian Food Legends Retold*.

Veena teaches English as a second language. Her writing has appeared in Canadian literary magazines and anthologies, and her book reviews have been published in *Herizons*, *Montréal Serai*, and the *Montreal Review of Books*. She curates an annual event — the Garden of Literary Delights — that spotlights Canadian writers of South Asian origin for the Kabir Centre, Montreal.

Having lived in ten cities across three countries, she now calls Tiohtià:ke (Montreal) home.